"Shavonne, can you—will you—forgive me?" Slade asked.

She heard the hopeful note in his voice, saw the expectant glimmer in his eyes. He fully expected her to say yes, she thought.

"I don't know if I want to forgive you," she said slowly. "You're telling me you didn't mean to treat me the way you did last time, that you're someone else now. Is it so easy for you to change your story, change your personality, to tell me what you think I want to hear?"

Something exploded inside him. Hearing her echo his own self-doubts triggered a wild storm of emotions—remorse and sorrow, frustration and confusion—and he couldn't think clearly. He could only react, and his reaction was all primitive male.

His hand snaked out and grabbed her wrist and pulled her to him. Before she could protest, his mouth closed hotly over hers. He kissed her with an urgent, greedy hunger.

Shavonne had no time to rally her defenses against his sensual assault. Overwhelmed by the taste, the touch and feel of him, she was helpless to stop her body's traitorous responses. . . .

WHAT ARE *LOVESWEPT* ROMANCES?

They are stories of true romance and touching emotion. We believe those two very important ingredients are constants in our highly sensual and very believable stories in the *LOVESWEPT* line. Our goal is to give you, the reader, stories of consistently high quality that may sometimes make you laugh, sometimes make you cry, but are always fresh and creative and contain many delightful surprises within their pages.

Most romance fans read an enormous number of books. Those they truly love, they keep. Others may be traded with friends and soon forgotten. We hope that each *LOVESWEPT* romance will be a treasure—a "keeper." We will always try to publish

LOVE STORIES YOU'LL NEVER FORGET
BY AUTHORS YOU'LL ALWAYS REMEMBER

The Editors

LOVESWEPT® • 207

Barbara Boswell
Playing Hard to Get

BANTAM BOOKS
TORONTO • NEW YORK • LONDON • SYDNEY • AUCKLAND

PLAYING HARD TO GET

A Bantam Book / September 1987

If you would be interested in receiving protective vinyl covers for your Loveswept books, please write to this address for information:

Loveswept
Bantam Books
P.O. Box 985
Hicksville, NY 11802

ISBN 0-553-21832-8

Published simultaneously in the United States and Canada

One

"I told you the plan was a mistake." Slade Ramsey had to shout to make himself heard over the raucous din of his family's voices. As usual, everyone in the Ramsey family had an opinion and none of them were the least bit hesitant in voicing it. Loudly and forcibly.

"I said it was a mistake from the very beginning," Slade repeated, pounding a fist on the table for emphasis.

An attention-grabbing device was essential in dealing with a roomful of Ramseys. Quentin, the father, had an engraved gavel he used for pounding; Radford, the firstborn son, slammed books; Vanessa, the only daughter, screamed and threw china. The other Ramseys, mother Nola, and Slade, Jed, and Ricky, second, third, and fourth born sons, respectively, had to pound shoes or fists, break pencils, or find some other props to make their points.

"It *was* a good plan," Rad snapped, glaring at his younger brother. "Except you botched it! All you had to do was charm Great-Aunt Augusta into selling you that piece of land and you blew it!"

Slade met his brother's icy steel-gray eyes without flinching. His own eyes, a bluish-gray, the color of slate, flashed with anger. "Great-Aunt Augusta may have chosen to live in a little West Virginia hick town, but she was pure Ramsey. Tough and cynical and stubborn as a goat. She wasn't about to be charmed by the grandson of her late, unlamented brother. She wouldn't hear of me buying the land from her, but she agreed to will it to me after she died. It was the best I could do, the only concession anyone could've gotten from her. Including you, Rad."

"Well, someone else did a helluva lot better in the charm and concession departmentt when it came to dealing with our recently departed great-aunt," Rad said coldly. He snatched the typewritten letter and notarized legal document from the table. "A Miss S-i-o-b-h-a-n Brady." He snorted. "What kind of un-American name is S-i-o-b-h-a-n, anyway?"

"It's pronounced Sh'vawn," Slade said quietly. "Accent on the second syllable. It's an Irish name, but she switched to a phonetic spelling when she started school. Except in legal documents, she uses S-h-a-v-o-n-n-e."

"You know her?" Quentin asked quickly, giving his second son a long, assessing stare.

Slade composed his features into a cool, unreadable mask. "I met her when I was in Star City to buy the land from Great-Aunt Augusta."

"To *try* to buy the land," Rad corrected him with a disgusted scowl. "You didn't succeed, remember? She gave us her permission to build on her portion of the land, and that's all. That's why we're in this mess."

"I don't remember you ever mentioning a Shavonne Brady, Slade." Quentin's smoke-gray eyes were fixed on Slade. "You never gave us any reason to believe that someone stood between us and that land. After she'd granted us permission to build, it seemed logical to assume that Augusta would will the land to her only surviving relatives. I never questioned you on that point."

"Which is why we went ahead and built the Ramsey Park Mall on Ramsey land outside of Houston," Rad said, clenching and unclenching his fists. "On the land we boys inherited from Granddaddy, fully expecting that the one-quarter of the property that we didn't own would be willed to us in time by Granddaddy's sister."

"May she rest in peace," Jed put in wryly.

Vanessa giggled. Quentin scowled disapprovingly at them and all attention focused back on Slade and Rad.

"Who is this Shavonne Brady, Slade?" Quentin asked. "What kind of hold did she have over Augusta?"

"No hold at all, unless you count sentiment," Slade said. "The Brady family lived next door to Great-Aunt Augusta. They were friends and neighbors for years."

"And you didn't have even a clue that these ingratiating neighbors were a threat to our claim?" Rad demanded incredulously.

"They weren't ingratiating neighbors," Slade said. "The Bradys knew Great-Aunt Augusta as a retired school teacher, living on her pension and her social security checks. She never mentioned her connection to us. When I arrived there, she introduced me as the grandson of her only brother Harlan, the brother she'd never liked, from the day he was born to the day he died. That's all the Bradys know about the Ramseys," he added, staring sightlessly into space.

Nola Ramsey spoke for the first time. "Slade, are you telling us that Shavonne Brady doesn't know she's one-quarter owner of the Ramsey Park Mall?"

Vanessa gasped. "She doesn't know she's inherited one-fourth of the newest, 100-million-dollar,

1.5-million-square-foot, state-of-the-art shopping mall?"

"When I visited Star City two years ago," Slade said slowly, "Shavonne Brady was a twenty-one-year-old student at West Virginia University in Morgantown, which borders Star City. She'd assumed legal guardianship of her four younger sisters when she was eighteen, the year their mother died. The Bradys consider Morgantown the ultimate urban experience. They know nothing about big business or Ramsey & Sons Development Corporation. And the lawyer, Judea Davison, the one who wrote this letter, was Great-Aunt Augusta's attorney. He's about seventy-nine years old and semi-retired. He's not about to investigate the value of the property."

"This is too good to be true!" Vanessa said enthusiastically. "We're dealing with an unsophisticated bunch of hillbilly orphans. No contest for even the youngest Ramsey!"

Everyone's eyes turned briefly to eighteen-year-old Ricky whose short dark hair stood on end, moussed into stiff spikes. The youngest Ramsey, wearing dark wraparound sunglasses, a brilliant orange shirt, and a pair of equally vivid jams shorts, was plugged into a set of headphones and paying no attention to the uproar going on around him.

"Point taken," Jed said dryly. "So this particular Brady bunch thinks Morgantown, West Virginia, is life in the fast lane?" He snickered and shook his head. "Wait till the li'l ole mountain gal finds out she's inherited a twenty-five-million-dollar piece of Ramsey & Sons' latest project!"

"She's not going to find out," Quentin said with steely finality. "Slade, I want you to go to Star City and offer to buy the property from Shavonne Brady—before she learns what's on it."

Slade felt himself grow cold inside. See Shavonne

again? "No, I can't do that," he said, speaking his thoughts aloud.

Quentin frowned. "You can't?" he repeated incredulously. "Or you won't?" He appeared stunned by his son's refusal. As chairman of the Houston-based privately owned mall development and management empire, which had created more than 125 shopping facilities in 30 states, Quentin Ramsey was not a man accustomed to being refused. Particularly not by his amiable son, Slade.

"Both," Slade said, meeting and holding his father's gaze. Slade was fully aware of his reputation as the "nice Ramsey," the considerate, trustworthy "good guy." He knew that was why he'd been the one originally sent to charm old Aunt Augusta into selling her land. His family viewed him as the quintessential nice guy. He was not a rattlesnake-chip off the old block like Rad or an irreverent smart aleck like Jed. Much to the Ramseys' collective disappointment.

"You can't and you won't?" Quentin asked. He did not look pleased. "Nola." He turned to his wife. "Will you please explain to your son exactly what is at stake here? *A stranger from a backwoods West Virginia town has just become part-owner of our most expensive, exclusive mall to date!* And *your* son—"

Nola smiled, undaunted by her husband's ire. "They're always *my* sons when they don't jump to your command."

"Slade spent all last month in California, supervising the new San Diego mini-mall complex, Daddy," Vanessa piped up. "Maybe he doesn't want to leave Lexie again so soon. She was awfully upset that he missed the Rutherford wedding and she had to go alone. And the Doeblers' party is next week. Lexie's likely to throw a fit if Slade misses that, too."

"Lexie Madison's temper tantrums are a thing of the past as far as Slade is concerned," Rad said.

"Slade's no longer a wimp. He knows how to handle women. Lexie doesn't dare step out of line these days."

"Lexie Madison is a bitch." This was from Ricky who'd removed his headphones and temporarily ze-roed in on the conversation. "She ought to be dating you, Rad, not a nice guy like Slade."

"I'm no longer Mr. Nice Guy, Rick," Slade said. There was a harsh edge to his voice, making him sound as hard as his father Quentin, as cold as his older brother Rad, as cynical as his younger brother Jed. "Haven't you noticed?"

Ricky shrugged. "You're always nice to me."

"Ah, but not to women," Vanessa said brightly. "After years of finishing last as a nice guy, Slade finally woke up and changed into the exciting kind of risky, elusive man that women can't resist. An irresistible Mr. Wrong. Lexie's running off to the Caribbean with that actor just a few weeks before her and Slade's wedding finally brought about the change, didn't it, Slade?"

Slade smiled tightly. "That did it, all right."

Vanessa grinned at him with sisterly approval. "Remember that night, Slade? I told you that Lexie said you were too dependable and thoughtful, too tame and predictable. And you vowed then and there to change. We both got plastered on margaritas and you decided to treat women the way Rad and Jed did. To be the kind of suave heartbreaker that women are always weeping over in *Cosmopolitan*. That was . . . when? About two years ago?"

"Two years and two months ago," he corrected her tersely. "Right before I went to Star City." Where he'd met Shavonne Brady and decided to try out his all new personality. On her . . .

Slade frowned as he felt the unpleasant chill that inevitably pervaded him when he remembered the way he'd treated Shavonne Brady.

At the time he'd attempted to justify his actions to himself by figuring that a woman who fell for the lines he'd spun for Shavonne deserved exactly what she got. He'd told himself that he was all through with his Eagle Scout virtues. Forget about the Golden Rule. All of that was obviously passé when it came to man-woman relationships.

Two years later, he was *still* trying to justify his actions to himself. With a depressing lack of success.

He allowed his mind to drift back to the first time he'd seen Shavonne Brady, standing on the porch of her house, next door to Great-Aunt Augusta's small frame home in Star City. Her image seemed to be indelibly etched in his memory . . .

Her thick blond hair, the color of wheat, had been pulled up into a bouncy ponytail, and her big, brown velvet eyes were fringed with long, dark lashes. She'd been wearing a yellow and white gingham sundress and her nubile young body was enticingly feminine, all golden and slender and shapely. She was small boned and delicate, just a quarter inch under five-feet-four. And her smile . . . It had hit him with the force of a lightning bolt. She was lovely, fresh, and natural. Her great dark eyes were devoid of all guile. He was soon to learn that she was a full ten years younger than he—and a virgin.

Slade had known he had no business going near her, but he had wanted her. And why shouldn't he take her? the ruthless new Slade had argued with his trustworthy old self. Wasn't the family credo "Whatever a Ramsey wants, a Ramsey gets"? It was about time he started living it. Especially since he was no longer a nice guy . . .

He'd deliberately set out to seduce her. Shavonne, innocent, inexperienced, and naive, had been no match for him. She'd fallen hard for him, as he'd meant for her to do.

And he'd treated her badly, dazzling her with his

charm to ensnare her, alternating periods of closeness and warmth with distance and withdrawal.
He'd used the tactics of a charming rat—beguiling
seduction, sweet lies, promises made only to be broken. He'd set her up to bring her down.

Shame coursed through him. The memory of the
terrible pain in Shavonne's eyes when he'd coolly
announced that he was returning to Texas after their
monthlong affair, haunted him still. He'd returned
to a frenetic social whirl in Houston that didn't ease
his guilt. Nothing did, not the string of affairs he'd
had, not even Lexie's avid renewed interest in him.

He'd coolly set out to woo his errant fiancée, using
the smooth operator charm he'd cultivated. Lexie
had responded to him as she never had before, con-
firming his grim theory that women preferred elusive heartbreakers to nice guys. He'd had the satisfaction of watching Lexie scheme to win him back,
and he kept her on edge, never letting her know
where she stood with him. He knew she loved every
tormenting minute of it.

His conscience never smote him for the games he
played with Lexie and the others, for he was careful
to play by the rules, to stay away from sweet young
girls who fell in love and had their hearts broken.
Except for that one-time lapse. In Star City, with
Shavonne Brady.

Why couldn't he forget Shavonne? he wondered
bleakly. Why did he still think of her at odd hours of
the day and night? And why had he thought of
contacting her a thousand times, only to feel himself freeze as he lifted the telephone receiver from its
cradle?

If he had the answers to those questions, perhaps
he could answer another one, he mused darkly. Why
wasn't he happy? His success with women rivaled
that of his brothers. The once-unattainable Lexie
Madison described herself as "mad about him."

He had it all, he assured himself, not for the first time. He was successful in business and successful in romance. So why was he plagued with this vague and ever-present dissatisfaction? And why did his insides churn whenever he thought of Star City—and Shavonne?

"Then, it's all settled." His mother's voice penetrated his bleak reverie. "Slade is going to Star City to buy back Augusta's land."

He was about to refuse, then he reconsidered. Perhaps he needed to see Shavonne again to finally exorcise her from his mind. She probably never gave him a thought; she'd undoubtedly put the memories of her first affair far behind her. But he needed to know that. He needed to make peace with her . . .

And then? He shrugged. The future was wide open. He was no longer a nice guy who finished last.

"'Bye, Mrs. Kelly, 'bye, Maura!" Shavonne Brady stood at the gate of the white-washed fence and waved to the young woman and toddler in the bright blue van that was pulling out of the mud and stone driveway.

"Is everybody gone?" asked sixteen-year-old Colleen, who'd joined her sister in the yard.

Shavonne nodded. "The Brady Day Nursery has survived another week."

"Think we'll survive Carrie Beth's birthday party tomorrow afternoon? We'll have a mob of kids here for that," Colleen reminded her with a smile.

Shavonne's gaze flickered to the small frame house next door, and sudden tears filled her eyes. "It's sad Aunt Augusta isn't going to be here. Remember what a kick she got out of Carrie Beth's birthday party last year?"

"When Carrie Beth stuck both hands in the cake,"

Colleen said, her smile becoming tremulous, "and smeared icing all over herself."

"I guess she won't do that this year, since she's a big girl of three," Shavonne said rather wistfully.

Their attention was diverted by the appearance of a gray Buick slowly winding along the narrow road that dead-ended at the Brady house. There were only two houses on the unpaved, gravel road high in the hills of rural Star City. The Bradys lived in one and the late Augusta Ramsey had lived in the other.

"Wonder who that is," Colleen mused. Stray cars were seldom seen along their secluded little lane. "All the nursery kids have been picked up."

"Probably some poor soul who's gotten himself lost on the way to Morgantown," Shavonne said. Then she went rigid, for even at a distance, she recognized the driver of the car.

"Colleen," she said, forcing herself to keep her voice steady, "why don't you go inside and help Erin get the kids ready for dinner? I'll . . . uh, give the lost driver directions and then come in."

"Okay," Colleen agreed cheerfully, and walked toward the house, not giving the car and driver another thought.

Colleen hadn't recognized the man behind the wheel, Shavonne thought. She was relieved at that. Facing Slade Ramsey again was going to be difficult enough without the added strain of an audience.

She watched the car steadily approach and the tension in her body increased. The blood drained from her face and she suddenly shivered, although the September evening was warm and balmy. Slade Ramsey. His name reverberated in her head. She had thought she would never see him again and had reconciled herself to that fact long ago. She didn't want to see him; he meant pain and trouble and misery. She drew in a deep breath. It was imperative to get rid of Slade Ramsey as quickly as possible.

He pulled his car into the narrow driveway and got out. She remained standing by the gate, and another shiver ran through her as he walked toward her. He hadn't changed much. His shoulders seemed broader, his tall frame a bit more muscular. Maybe there were a few lines around his slate-colored eyes that hadn't been there two years and two months ago.

Slade wasn't movie-star handsome, but he had a compelling masculinity that had never failed to stir her senses. Even now, feelings she'd managed to repress since his abrupt departure sparked to life within her. She tensed, refusing to acknowledge the tingling in her abdomen, the tightness in her breasts.

Her gaze swept compulsively over him. He was definitely an attractive man. The dark, thick hair. The dark brows and dark lashes that heightened the impact of his light eyes. The sharp blade of a nose and firm, square jaw. His mouth was frankly sensual, the lower lip fuller than the upper one.

She remembered the feel of those lips on hers, on every pleasure point of her body, and her pulses leaped. She remembered the way her heart had sung whenever he'd bestowed one of his infrequent smiles upon her. His mouth definitely qualified as a danger zone to her.

"Hello, Slade." She congratulated herself for being the first to speak. And for the steadiness of her voice. She'd managed to mask her involuntary attraction. She was in full control of herself, quite unlike the young Shavonne that Slade Ramsey had known. His abrupt desertion of her had irrevocably changed her from a girl into a woman.

"Hello, Shavonne." Slade was startled that his voice shook. His hands were shaking too. He fought to overcome the emotions that suddenly welled up inside him at the sight of her.

She was even prettier than he remembered. Her

beautiful pale blond hair fell nearly to her shoulders in a thick curtain, and she no longer had the bangs that she'd often run her fingers through in a nervous gesture he'd found endearing. Her chocolate-brown eyes were huge and dominated her heart-shaped face. His eyes fastened on her mouth, soft and pink and alluring, and he felt an involuntary tightening in his loins.

She was wearing blue jeans and a bright yellow cotton sweater that clung lovingly to her mature, rounded breasts. Her waist was small, her hips gently sloping, her legs long and slender. His mind superimposed an image of her lying naked in his arms, and he caught his breath.

"It's been a long time," he said, and nearly groaned at his lack of originality. Smiling sheepishly, he added, "I've gone over this scene a thousand times in my head and thought of an equal amount of openings—only to come up with one of the oldest clichés on record. It would serve me right if you were to reply, 'not nearly long enough.' "

Shavonne eyed him warily. What was this, some new line? she wondered. Did he actually expect her to believe that the ever-cool Slade Ramsey was nervous about seeing her again? Well, she wasn't falling for it. She kept her voice faultlessly polite as she asked, "What brings you to Star City, Slade?"

Slade stared at her, nonplussed by her mannerly indifference. She was cool, calm, and controlled, something she'd never been around him before. Her face, always so open and expressive, was now a closed book. Her eyes, which in the past had reflected unfailingly whatever emotions she was feeling, were veiled. Where she'd once been an exuberant girl, young for her twenty-one years, she now appeared a restrained twenty-three year old woman, mature beyond her age.

"You look wonderful, Shavonne," he said, and wondered why he felt the compulsion to smash through her guarded reserve. He smiled at her, turning on the full force of the Ramsey smile, designed to charm and disarm men and women alike.

Shavonne raised her brows slightly. Unlike before, she now recognized the insincere smile of a master manipulator when she saw it. She congratulated herself on her insight, and decided to come straight to the point. "I take it you received Mr. Davison's letter concerning your Great-Aunt Augusta's will?" There could be no other reason why he'd come here, and she wasn't about to delude herself into thinking otherwise.

"As you know," she continued, "Aunt Augusta left me her house and its contents. We've taken a few pieces of furniture, along with some of her personal belongings—specifically, her chiming mantle clock and her collection of china elephants. They have sentimental value to my sisters and me, although I don't think they have much financial worth."

Her words swirled around Slade's head. She was addressing him with all the emotion of an estate-planning adviser, he thought. She was looking through him as if they were casual strangers who'd just met today. As if she hadn't given her virginity to him, hadn't cried in his arms with the ecstasy of her first climax. As if she hadn't once been passionately in love with him.

"There are a number of old family photographs that you might find interesting," she continued blandly. "I boxed them all up. Please feel free to take them if you'd like. And to go through Aunt Augusta's house and take anything else you want from it."

Her gaze flickered to the old frame house on the other side of the fence, and her eyes softened. "We still miss her a lot. It's hard to believe that she isn't in her kitchen right now, baking something for dessert. Aunt Augusta had quite a sweet tooth, you know."

"No, I didn't," he said flatly. "I knew very little about her, except that she and my grandfather maintained a lifelong feud. I only visited her once and spent most of that month with you, not with Great-Aunt Augusta."

He felt an odd satisfaction that two spots of color pinked Shavonne's cheeks. But she didn't rise to the bait he'd cast. Instead, she made her voice even more colorless and unemotional, if that was possible.

"We offered to contact you when Aunt Augusta's health began to fail a few months ago, but she absolutely refused to let us do it. She didn't want to see you or any other member of your family . . ." Shavonne shrugged and let her voice trail off.

There was a brief moment of silence.

Slade was the first to break it. "The letter from Davison didn't mention her cause of death," he murmured awkwardly.

"It was listed as congestive heart failure," Shavonne said. "She was eighty-seven years old, and Doctor Pratt said her heart and lungs just plain wore out." She blinked back a rush of tears. "Aunt Augusta was at home when she died. She didn't want any part of any hospital. My sisters and I took turns staying with her. We were all with her—at the end."

"I see."

Another awkward moment of silence descended. "I didn't mean to ramble on like that," Shavonne said at last.

"No one close to me has ever died," Slade said, "except my grandfather, and I was just a child then. I can't imagine being at someone's deathbed. I admire you for staying with Great-Aunt Augusta . . . through it all."

Their eyes met and held.

Shavonne, he thought, and suddenly, shockingly,

he began to ache. She had been so young and sweet with him, so loving and warm and beautiful. And now she was looking at him with eyes as chilled and wary as a consumer advocate agent investigating a fraudulent advertising claim.

Shavonne tore her gaze from his. Something in his eyes was making her uneasy. He was staring at her in a way he never had before. She couldn't identify his expression, but she knew she'd never seen it during the month they'd spent as lovers.

She thought of the roller coaster highs and lows of their monthlong affair, of the devastating pain she'd felt when it ended. But she was strong now, and at peace with herself. She would never, ever risk her hard-won strength and serenity for the dangers to be found in a pair of seductive gray eyes.

"I'll get the key to Aunt Augusta's house," she said briskly. The sooner he was gone, the better. "Wait here and I'll bring it out to you." She turned and started toward the house.

"May I come in?" he asked quietly.

She stopped in her tracks. "I'd rather you didn't."

"It's ironic, isn't it?" His shrug was self-deprecating. "The last time I was here, I declined all your invitations to come inside and meet your sisters. Now, when I'd like an invitation, one isn't forthcoming."

She looked at him blankly. "I'm suppressing the urge to say something truly trite, along the lines of 'that's the way the cookie crumbles.' "

"Glad you suppressed it." He flashed a grin, then immediately sobered. "But 'he reaps what he sows' is completely apropos."

It shamed him to remember that two years ago he'd sat in his rental car outside her house arrogantly honking the horn to summon her. He'd never bothered to go to her door to collect her, never bothered to acquaint himself with her family.

Shavonne was remembering, too, remembering

how she'd come running eagerly at his imperious summons, so thrilled to be with him that she hadn't given his lack of courtesy a thought. She shuddered and their gazes locked.

"I thought I was being cool," he said wryly. "Super macho. I was determined that no one was going to accuse me of being a gentleman."

"There wasn't a chance of that," she assured him. Still, there was the time they'd found a lost child crying in the supermarket where they'd gone to buy some snacks. Slade had comforted the little boy and taken him to the store manager, then had stayed with the child until his mother claimed him. Shavonne remembered thinking what a kind and gentle man he was.

She'd thought she'd seen a glimpse of a truly nice person beneath his cool-guy persona other times as well. Once he'd stopped his car to rescue a terrified puppy that was crouching, frozen with fear, in the middle of the road. He'd read the tags on the pup's collar, driven it to the address listed, and refused the grateful owner's offer of a reward. Another time he'd bought a whole book of raffle tickets from an elderly man selling them to raise money for a church trip.

Those displays of generosity had made her love him all the more. She'd thought if she was sweet and patient, that side of his character would fully emerge. Well, she'd been wrong, she told herself flatly as she went into the house to find the key. It hadn't.

She returned a few moments later and handed him the key. "Just drop it in our mailbox when you're ready to leave," she instructed him coolly. "I assume you're staying in Morgantown tonight."

He'd rented a motel room there during his last stay in West Virginia. Room 315 at the Ramada Inn. She knew she would never forget it. She'd spent too much time in it with the man she'd loved, the man who hadn't loved her. She flinched at the memory and withdrew further into herself.

"Yes," he said absently. "I'm staying in Morgantown."

She studied him. He was staring at her so strangely, turning the key over in his hand. She couldn't even begin to guess what was going on with him, but then, that was nothing new. She had always been remarkably inept at reading Slade Ramsey. Neither she nor her sisters understood anything about men. Men were alien, exotic creatures who had never been a part of the Brady girls' lives.

Suddenly, a light dawned, and Shavonne knew why Slade Ramsey had come back.

Two

"The land!" Shavonne exclaimed. Slade's startled expression confirmed her insight. "That's why you came to Star City that first time, to buy Aunt Augusta's little piece of land in Texas. She didn't want to sell it to you then, and it was willed to me along with her house."

"The land," Slade repeated dumbly. Good Lord, he thought. He'd been so absorbed in his thoughts of Shavonne, he'd actually forgotten about that infernal piece of land!

"This time you've come to buy it from me," she said.

"Shavonne," he began unsteadily. According to Ramsey plans, he was now supposed to cheat Shavonne out of her inheritance.

An inheritance she had earned by being a lifelong friend and neighbor to a lonely old woman. Slade was overcome by a flood of self-loathing. He'd come a long, long way from the nice guy who'd had his heart broken by a shallow, thrill-seeking woman. And he'd come an even longer way from the young Eagle Scout who'd been cited for his moral character.

He blinked in wonder. He felt as if he were slowly waking up from a weird trance, one that had lasted two years and two months and in which he had said and done things totally alien to his very soul. His blood roared in his head as he stared into Shavonne's remote brown eyes.

He couldn't do it, he realized, and a strange, almost exultant feeling coursed through him, catapulting him out of the twilight zone he'd inhabited these past few years. He wouldn't do it. He was *not* going to buy that land from Shavonne.

"How much are you prepared to offer?" she asked. Oh, it all made sense to her now, she thought. Slade's unexpected arrival coupled with his uncharacteristic nervousness—his unease around her, those peculiar glances he kept giving her. He was trying to assess when and how to bring up the subject of Aunt Augusta's land. And he was undoubtedly worried that she wouldn't sell it to him.

She decided to set the record straight at once. "I'm willing to sell the land to you. It means nothing to me. I'll never go to Texas."

He clenched his jaw and his Adam's apple bobbed as he visibly swallowed hard. "You didn't think I'd sell it to you, did you?" she continued. "You thought I would deliberately hang on to it—for revenge." It was wonderful to finally face Slade Ramsey as a mature and sophisticated woman, she decided as a thrill ran through her. To confront him instead of being manipulated by him.

"Shavonne, you don't understand."

"Oh, I think I do. I'm not quite the nitwit you think I am." She couldn't help but smile with pride. For the first time ever, she'd caught him off-guard. "You came here determined to buy the land and equally certain that I wouldn't sell it. You have a clever strategy all mapped out to get it. What you never expected was that I'd come right out and ask you point blank if you wanted to buy it. And that I'd agree to sell it to you straight out."

She looked so pleased with herself that Slade fought the urge to smile. Her obvious delight at having outsmarted the big bad wolf struck him as amusing and endearing.

Shavonne saw the glimmer of amusement in his eyes and froze. Was he laughing at her? She knew he thought she was stupid, a worthless nothing. He'd certainly treated her that way in the past. Her jubilation ended. "How much were you preparing to offer for the land?" she asked coldly.

"Shavonne, I don't want to talk about the land right now."

"But I do," she insisted.

"Shavonne, I want you to listen to—"

She bristled at the note of authority in his tone. "I don't take orders from you, Slade Ramsey. And I won't play those treacherous little games you love so much. So you can forget all about whatever scheme you dreamed up to get the land and tell me right now how much you were supposed to offer me for it."

His face reddened. The sum that Ramsey & Sons Development Corporation was preparing to give her for her share of the twenty-five-million-dollar mall complex was extremely low. Criminally low. Immorally low. He was acutely ashamed of himself and his family. They were nothing better than a band of ruthless swindlers, heartlessly bent on cheating a sweet and loyal young woman out of what was rightfully hers. No, he reiterated to himself. He wasn't going to be a party to it, whatever his father and brothers might say or do.

"You're stalling, Slade. How much?"

He could merely tell her the sum, he thought. He didn't have to go through with the sale.

"How much?" Shavonne pressed when he hesitated. So this was the way to handle men like Slade Ramsey? she marveled, awed by her sudden success. You talked tough and didn't back off—totally opposite to the way she'd dealt with Slade when she'd been in love with him. Then she'd been conciliatory and eager to please. She'd been glad to sacrifice or compromise or do whatever it took to make him happy.

And it hadn't worked. He'd treated her like the weak fool he'd considered her to be. She folded her arms in front of her chest. "Well?" she demanded.

"Twenty-five thousand dollars," Slade said softly.

Shavonne barely managed to suppress a gasp. "Twenty-five thousand dollars?" A veritable fortune! Mr. Davison had told her that Aunt Augusta's house might bring them as much as twelve or thirteen thousand dollars, and she and her sisters had been flabbergasted at that heady sum. But this! Twenty-five thousand dollars for a piece of land in Texas that she'd never seen, that she didn't care if she ever did see?

She stared at him, dazed. "I must admit, I'm surprised," she confessed. "I would have thought a man like you would've offered me the lowest possible price for the land. Yet here you are, offering me twenty-five thousand dollars for it."

She was bewildered. Was it possible for a man to be unscrupulous when it came to women and love, but impeccably honest in his business dealings? She knew even less about businessmen than she did about men in love, she thought uneasily. But twenty-five thousand dollars . . .

"I accept your offer," she said, before he could change his mind. "The land is yours. What do we do next? Get a lawyer to write up a bill of sale? I can call Mr. Davison right away."

Slade pressed a hand over his eyes. Lord, what a dilemma! He could return to Houston tomorrow with the deed in his hand, and his father and brothers would hail him as a hero. Ramsey & Sons would have an additional twenty-five million dollars for its coffers and full control of Ramsey Park Mall. And Shavonne Brady would be delighted with the deal. Her stunned and overjoyed reaction to the twenty-five-thousand-dollar sum made him wince.

"Shavonne . . ." He paused and drew in a deep breath. She was as innocent and naive as a baby in such matters. However low he might have sunk these past years, he hadn't yet reached the point where he could cheat her—or anyone—this way.

"I want to sell," she said. "But I won't accept a dime less than twenty-five thousand dollars."

"Now what?" he murmured aloud, and groaned. How was he supposed to tell her that such a deal made him a pirate, robbing her of a fortune? How did he tell her that her land was worth an astonishing twenty-five *million* dollars when she thought twenty-five *thousand* was a kingly sum? She wouldn't believe him. She would assume he was trying to flummox her. She didn't trust him as it was.

Shavonne was on the verge of pleading with him to buy the land. She and her sisters were forever struggling to make ends meet, and the prospect of so much money seemed like a dream come true.

Then she thought of the days when she and Slade had been lovers. Pleading with him would catapult her right back into subservience. They would be assuming their former roles of master and supplicant. No, she thought, never again. The Bradys would manage somehow, but she would never ask Slade Ramsey for anything.

"Of course," she said, "if you don't want to buy the land, I'm not about to force it on you." She hoped she managed to pull off a credible shrug of indifference.

Playing it cool was very, very difficult for her. She'd always been open; she hadn't known how to be anything else. Then Slade Ramsey had come along and taught her that a woman must be secretive and deceptive to survive in the world of men. She'd decided then and there that she didn't have what it took to get and keep a man, and had withdrawn into her safe world inhabited by comfortingly familiar females.

She was suddenly weary and depressed and utterly exhausted. It had been a shock to see Slade again. Keeping her feelings under control while attempting to match his sophistication and poise was proving to be an intolerable strain.

"I'm going inside now," she said. "Perhaps we can discuss the sale of the land some other time."

As if on cue, her youngest sister, fifteen-year-old Megan, hollered through the screen door, "Dinnertime, Shavonne!"

"I have to go." Shavonne turned and rushed toward the house.

Slade automatically followed her. They'd reached the bottom of the porch steps when the screen door burst open and a little girl with dark brown eyes and long blond curls ran onto the old wooden porch. She started carefully down the wide steps toward Shavonne.

"Dinnertime, Shavonne," the little girl shrieked importantly.

"I'm coming, Carrie Beth." Shavonne scooped the child up in her arms and settled her on her hip.

Slade smiled at the appealing picture they made. The little girl was so clearly a Brady, with her petite frame and blond hair and dark brown eyes.

"Who's this little lady?" he asked, reaching out to touch one of the girl's long curls. The child drew back and clung to Shavonne, turning her head away from him.

He was disconcerted by the child's rejection. Children and dogs usually liked him, no doubt sensing his inherent "nice-guyness." Terrific, he thought glumly. All the Bradys hated him, even the littlest ones.

"This is my niece," Shavonne said tightly, inching up the stairs in an obvious attempt to escape.

"How old are you, sweetie?" he asked, determined to win a positive response from the child. Making friends with anyone connected to Shavonne was suddenly of the highest importance to him.

The little girl carefully kept her head averted, but extended her hand and raised three small fingers. He chuckled, genuinely charmed. "Three years old? Now, let me guess. Your name is Carrie Beth."

The child turned to face him in astonishment. "My name *is* Carrie Beth," she said shyly.

"And I'm Slade. I'm pleased to meet you, Carrie Beth."

"Oh, please!" Shavonne sighed impatiently. "What game are you playing this time, Slade?"

"I'm not playing games, Shavonne." He was grateful for his small victory. She was still here, still talking to him. "Which one of your sisters is Carrie Beth's mother? I seem to recall one of them being married, but I don't remember who."

"I'm not surprised," she said coolly. "You weren't interested in hearing about my family, you never listened when I mentioned them. You always looked incredibly bored whenever I tried to discuss anything of personal interest to me."

It was true, he admitted grimly to himself. It had all been part of his game plan to keep things light and superficial, to keep an emotional distance between them. Shavonne, in her inexperience, had assumed that he found her boring. Regret coursed through him. She had tried so hard to please him, to entertain him, to be whatever he wanted her to be. "You never bored me, Shavonne," he said quietly. "Not once, not ever."

He could tell she didn't believe him. Her arms

tightened around Carrie Beth, then she turned wordlessly and started up the stairs.

"I remember now!" he called as she reached the top step. "Erin is your married sister. She's a year younger than you and she married right out of high school. And I remember Carrie Beth now too. She was just an infant the last time I saw her. She's Erin's daughter."

Shavonne turned to stare at him, looking as surprised as he felt by his power of recall. Those facts had been stored in the recesses of his memory, proving that he must have been listening intently to her on a level he hadn't been aware of back then . . . and despite his determination not to. Quite a few of his brain cells held information about Shavonne Brady, he thought wryly. Seeing her again brought so much to the fore.

The front door suddenly swung open, and Shavonne was joined on the porch by a batallion of Bradys. Slade stared at the flock of brown-eyed blondes and wondered who was who. One sister held a baby girl who was dressed identically to Carrie Beth in red overalls and a candy-striped shirt.

"What's going on, Shavonne?" the young woman asked.

"Nothing, Erin," Shavonne replied tightly. "Mr. Ramsey was just leaving."

Slade studied the group huddled on the porch of the worn old house and was struck by a horrifying revelation. They looked like a poor family! Their clothes were clean and pressed, but were obviously, unmistakably inexpensive, as were their depressingly well-worn shoes. The Bradys could never afford to shop in the stores that graced the Ramsey fleet of malls, and the harsh realization nearly choked him.

Two years ago, he hadn't considered their lowly financial status. Nothing had had the power to touch him because he'd been totally self-absorbed, hugging his wounded pride around him like a cloak. He had used his own pain as a justification to hurt Shavonne. He could have allowed her love to soothe and heal the wounds inflicted by Lexie's rejection, but he'd chosen not to.

He was seized by the futile wish to somehow change the past, to make reparations for the pain he'd caused. "Shavonne, may I take you to dinner?" he asked quickly. "We need to talk . . ." His heart pounded with anticipation. He realized just how much he wanted to spend the evening with her. They did have to talk about the land. And then . . . His pulses quickened.

"No," she said flatly. "Please, just go away, Slade. We don't want you here. We don't need you."

He jammed his hands into his pockets and strode swiftly to his car. He didn't trust himself to remain with her for another minute, for he couldn't help remembering when she had clung to him and pleaded with him not to leave her. When she *had* wanted and needed him. The intensity of the bittersweet memory left him reeling.

"I'll be back tomorrow, Shavonne," he called as he opened the car door. He meant it as a promise.

Shavonne interpreted it as a threat. "I'd rather deal with you through my lawyer," she shouted back, hoping she sounded sufficiently litigious. Old Judea Davison might suffer from occasional memory lapses, but he certainly was capable of overseeing the sale of her land to Slade Ramsey. Then she wouldn't have to see Slade again. That was good, because when he turned those compelling blue-gray eyes on her, she started feeling things she shouldn't, started thinking foolish thoughts. . . .

Slade climbed into his car, and the resounding slam of the door and gunning of the engine jarred the peaceful country silence.

"That wasn't the man from the electric company,

was it?" Megan asked nervously as they watched Slade's car wind its way back up the road. "Are they threatening to turn us off again?"

"No one is going to turn off anything, Megan," Shavonne assured her youngest sister. "We worked out payment plans with all the utilities, remember?"

"I remember how creepy it was when they shut off the electricity," Megan said with a shiver.

"That won't happen again," Shavonne promised.

"So who's the man?" Megan asked. "He threatened to come back tomorrow."

"Shavonne, isn't that the man you used to . . . uh, love?" Tara, Shavonne's nineteen-year-old sister, asked hesitantly. "I remember seeing him a few times at Aunt Augusta's that summer he was visiting. He was so big and tall and he never smiled."

"That's him. Slade Ramsey." Shavonne sighed. "If I had had a lick of sense, I never would've gotten mixed up with him then. And now . . ." She stared anxiously at the horizon. "I don't know what he's up to now. If only I knew, maybe I could figure out what to do next."

"Did he come here to get back together with you?" Tara asked.

Shavonne shook her head. "He came to buy the land Aunt Augusta left us. He offered me twenty-five thousand dollars for it."

The sisters stared at each other in stunned silence, clearly overwhelmed at the sum. Colleen was the first to find her voice. "Oh, Shavonne!" she exclaimed, gasping. "I can't believe it! When will we get the money?"

"We never did get around to finalizing the terms," Shavonne said thoughtfully, and suddenly her expression turned to one of alarm. "I just hope I haven't ruined it. I'm afraid I might've said yes too quickly. I don't think I should have acted so eager to sell."

"Now he'll offer you less for the land," Colleen

predicted. "It's the theory of supply and demand. Mrs. Allen, our history teacher, was telling us about it in class last week. If you make something hard to get, the demand for it is greater. And you can demand more for it."

"It seems to work that way with men, too," Erin said grimly.

"Aunt Augusta was absolutely right when she told me to play hard to get with Slade," Shavonne mused aloud. Her cheeks burned when she thought of how swiftly, how easily she'd fallen into Slade's arms two years and two months ago. "But I was too self-deluded to listen to her."

"I remember Mama used to say that men only want what they can't have," Tara said.

"Do you think it's true, Shavonne?" Colleen asked.

Shavonne sighed. "I don't know, Colleen. Maybe it is."

"But maybe there are exceptions to the rule?" Colleen asked wistfully. "Do you think so, Shavonne?"

Shavonne laid her hand on her younger sister's shoulder. She'd once been a hopeful romantic like Colleen, believing that if she was warm and honest and caring, the man she loved would love her in return. It hadn't worked that way, though, not for her or for Erin or for their mother. But she couldn't bring herself to dash Colleen's girlish dreams.

"Maybe you'll find the exception to the rule, Colleen," she said gently. "I hope you will."

"Well, I'm not even going to look, not for a typical male or an exceptional one," Tara said with a trace of defiance. "Who needs a man and all the trouble he brings?"

"Not me," said Megan.

"Not me!" exclaimed Carrie Beth, and the five sisters laughed. Pleased at being the center of attention, the little girl added, "I'm glad that daddy go'd away. He scared Courtney."

The older Bradys glanced at one-year-old Courtney, placid and content in Erin's arms, and exchanged knowing smiles. The truth was little Courtney was fearless and her older sister Carrie Beth feared everything. Shavonne gave her small niece a fierce hug. "The man is gone, honey. Courtney has nothing to worry about and neither do you. Now"—she herded her sisters toward the door—"let's go in and eat our dinner."

"And talk about what to do with the twenty-five thousand dollars," Megan said enthusiastically.

"*If* we get it," amended ever-cautious Erin.

Tara grinned. "*When* we get it."

"How about *if* and *when* we get it?" Shavonne suggested, then felt compelled to add, "But don't get your hopes up." Slade Ramsey couldn't be counted on; no one knew that better than she.

Three

Later that evening, as Shavonne was helping Erin bathe Carrie Beth and Courtney, Megan burst into the bathroom, her dark eyes wide with excitement.

"Shavonne, you have a phone call," she said breathlessly. "Long distance, person-to-person from a Mr. Quentin Ramsey."

"Quentin Ramsey? Isn't that Aunt Augusta's awful nephew?" Erin asked.

Augusta Ramsey had never hesitated to speak scathingly of her late brother Harlan and his son, Quentin. From the Bradys' computations, the elderly woman had last seen her dreadful nephew in his cradle. They figured he must have made an incredibly bad impression on his aunt, for she continued to denounce him until her dying day.

Shavonne's hand was shaking as she lifted the telephone receiver to her ear. She knew Quentin Ramsey was Slade's father. Was it possible that Slade had already gotten in touch with him? She'd heard so many tales of the "thieving, conniving Ramseys" from Aunt Augusta, and she'd experienced her own misery at Slade's hands. She believed them capable of anything. Her heart pounded as she said hello to Quentin Ramsey.

"Have you had a visit from my son Slade, Miss Brady?" Quentin asked, a note of impatience in his tone.

"Yes, I have," she replied shakily.

"I take it Slade made an offer on the property you inherited from my late aunt, Augusta Ramsey?" His voice fairly dripped with contempt when he said his aunt's name.

"Yes, he did." She decided to tell him the sum, just in case Slade was thinking about lowering it. "He offered me twenty-five thousand dollars. But we haven't signed anything."

Before she could say another word, Quentin boomed, "No one is pressuring you to sell, Miss Brady. But allow me to encourage you. I'll up the price to fifty thousand."

"Fifty thousand *dollars*?" she repeated incredulously. Tara, Colleen, and Megan had gathered in the kitchen to listen, and their faces mirrored her shock.

Tara placed her hand firmly over the mouthpiece of the telephone receiver. "Tell him you'll think about it," she whispered. "Supply and demand, remember? Don't seem too eager to sell."

It was exceedingly difficult to react coolly to the prospect of fifty thousand dollars, but Shavonne followed Tara's advice. "I'll think about it," she told Quentin, knowing she sounded totally unconvincing.

She heard a muffled curse, then Quentin said, "Seventy-five thousand, then!" He sounded as if he were grinding his teeth.

"Seventy-five thousand?" she squeaked. She thought she might faint. Her sisters gasped collectively and stared at her, goggle-eyed.

Shavonne was about to answer yes, yes, yes! But Tara covered the mouthpiece again. "Tell him to call you back in the morning."

"I don't want to sound greedy," Shavonne protested in a whisper. "What if he says just to forget the whole thing?"

"If it's worth seventy-five thousand dollars to him tonight, it'll be worth it to him in the morning," Tara said.

"Remember what Aunt Augusta said," Colleen added. "Play hard to get."

Shavonne frowned. "It just doesn't seem right . . ."

Then she looked around the old kitchen, with its peeling wallpaper and ancient refrigerator, circa 1937, so old-fashioned that it didn't even have a freezer compartment, just two small shelves to hold two ice trays. And the old wood burning stove was becoming increasingly temperamental, to say nothing of the added inconvenience of having to keep a supply of wood on hand.

With seventy-five thousand dollars, they could have the kitchen repapered. They could buy a new stove and a new refrigerator. They could pay off their ever-mounting bills. She gazed at the eager, hopeful faces of her younger sisters. She was the head of the family, and she felt her responsibilities keenly.

"Mr. Ramsey, I'll think about your offer overnight," she said decisively into the phone. "Please call me tomorrow morning and I'll give you my answer."

Slade pulled his car into the Bradys' driveway shortly before ten the next morning. Maybe it was too early to pay a visit, but he'd been unable to wait any longer. He had been awake for hours. After a miserably restless night in his motel room in nearby Morgantown, he'd finally given up all hope of sleep and trudged over to the university track field at dawn to run until he could hardly stand.

But he could still think, and his thoughts continued to torture him. Images of Shavonne and her family ran incessantly through his mind.

As he stared at the Bradys' home, he felt his throat tighten, felt every nerve in his body tense. Could he ever make Shavonne see him as the man he really was, not the rat he'd pretended to be? He had to! he thought urgently. For his own peace of mind. He didn't allow himself to consider any other reason why Shavonne Brady's opinion of him should matter so intensely.

His heart began to pound as he walked onto the porch of the old house. The inside door was open and he knocked on the screen door.

One of the younger Bradys, a pretty girl with long hair curling around her shoulders, appeared at the door. "Hello," he said, and smiled, hoping to ease the wary suspicion in her eyes. "Which sister are you?" he asked pleasantly.

"Megan Brady. What do you want?"

"I'd like to see Shavonne, Megan. May I come in?"

Megan shook her head. "Shavonne's not here. She and Erin went into Morgantown to buy the balloons and stuff for Carrie Beth's birthday party this afternoon."

"Carrie Beth's birthday is today?"

"She's three today." Megan's voice trembled and she started to gnaw anxiously on her thumbnail. Slade noticed for the first time how nervous the teen-ager was. "Now please go away, Mr. Ramsey."

"Megan, there's nothing to be afraid of," he assured her in a soothing voice. "I just want to come in and wait for Shavonne."

"I can't let you in," she said bluntly. "I'm here alone with Carrie Beth and I'm not strong enough to stop you if you—if you should start hitting us."

Slade was appalled. "Hit you? I've never struck a child or a woman in my entire life! My God, what kind of a man do you think I am?"

"Just a man." Megan shrugged. "Erin's husband, Charlie Ray Tyler, used to hit her. And he tried to hit Carrie Beth, too, but Erin and Shavonne wouldn't let him. One time Charlie Ray broke Erin's arm."

Slade could hardly believe what he'd heard. He was horrified and outraged. "That's unpardonable! I hope to hell the bastard is behind bars!"

"Nope, even better." Megan smiled suddenly. His reaction seemed to have pleased her. "He's dead. Got knocked off his motorcycle and run over by a pickup truck. That was before Courtney was born, so he never got the chance to try and hurt her."

"Well, I imagine his funeral was one you all truly enjoyed."

She grinned. "You sound a lot like Aunt Augusta. She never liked Charlie Ray either. None of us did, especially when he would get drunk and beat up Erin. We were all scared to death of Charlie Ray."

"I can see why." Slade shook his head. It was a grim tale. As depressing as—his gaze flicked over the shabby porch—as this weather-beaten, run-down old house. Yet during their affair, Shavonne had been so bright and upbeat that he'd never thought of her as trapped in poverty, trying to hold her family together, knowing her sister was abused by her husband. Had he ever really known her at all? he wondered.

From inside the house came a thunderous crash and a high-pitched scream. Megan and Slade both started at the sound.

"Uh-oh!" The girl rushed off to investigate.

Slade tried the door. It was unlocked. He walked into the house, following the sound of the cries. An old metal floor lamp had been overturned and lay on the floor in the dilapidated front room.

Carrie Beth, wearing a blue and red plaid dress and bright blue tights, was crying hysterically. Megan picked her up and tried to soothe her.

"Is she hurt?" he asked.

Megan shook her head. "She's just scared. The loud noise scared her."

Carrie Beth stopped wailing long enough to glance at Slade, then she began to cry again in earnest.

"Carrie Beth's scared of you," Megan said. "She's scared of everything, although she's not as bad as she used to be."

"Poor little Carrie Beth," he said. "She's had a hard time, having a violent father and all." Perhaps if he kept Megan talking, she would forget he wasn't supposed to be inside.

"She has us," Megan said simply. "She'll be all right. Shavonne said so."

Slade smiled at the girl's complete confidence in her oldest sister. "How long have Erin and her children been living here with you?" he asked, wishing he could ask Shavonne. He found himself insatiably curious about her. He wanted to learn everything there was to know about her life—a life that most definitely included her family. He didn't bother to ponder his consuming interest in Shavonne Brady, but merely accepted it.

"They've been here two years," Megan answered. "Erin moved back after Charlie Ray broke her arm." She blushed suddenly and stared at the floor. Her voice was low. "Then she got pregnant with Courtney, and Charlie Ray got killed."

Courtney was the result of a failed attempt at a reconciliation, Slade guessed, wondering why any woman would even consider reconciling with a man who broke bones and threatened to assault babies. But Megan was clearly uncomfortable with the topic, so he didn't press further.

"It can't be easy, financially," he said, "with all seven of you to support."

"It sure isn't. There's never enough money! Shavonne and Erin run a day-care nursery here at home"—she nodded toward the playpens and toys that littered the room—"and we hardly ever buy anything, but we still run short every month."

"But why doesn't Shavonne get a teaching job? I know she was getting a degree in elementary education at the university. Surely she could find a teaching position that would pay more than baby-sitting?"

"Shavonne never finished at the university. She dropped out when Erin and Carrie Beth moved back in 'cause there wasn't enough money. And then Courtney was born and there really, *really* wasn't enough."

"But that's not fair," he said. "Shavonne had to give up her degree to support Erin and her two children?" *Along with the three younger Bradys*, he added silently.

Megan took instant offense. "Shavonne says that having Erin and Carrie Beth and Courtney safe and happy with us is worth a lot more than any old teaching degree." She glared at him, clutching Carrie Beth and looking remarkably like a junior edition of Shavonne.

Her words hit him with the force of a sledgehammer. He remembered how serious Shavonne had been about obtaining her degree. She'd been working at the university bookstore to pay her tuition, scheduling her classes around her work and sometimes her work around her classes. And she'd given up her education to make barely enough money to support her family by baby-sitting?

He could hardly fathom such a sacrifice. It was not a choice any Ramsey would have made. He'd never had to sacrifice anything for anyone, he realized thoughtfully. From the day he was born, he'd had whatever he wanted . . . except for when Lexie had jilted him.

And how had he reacted to that? He stared grimly into space. If Lexie's rejection of him had been one of life's tests of character, he'd flunked.

"Are you okay?" Megan asked. "You look kind of strange."

"I haven't been okay for quite a while," he said slowly. "But, you know, I think I'm finally on the way back." He smiled at Megan and the toddler in her arms. "Do you mind if I wait here for Shavonne? It's very important that I see her."

Megan considered it. "I guess so," she said at last. "Carrie Beth and I were looking at the photo album. She loves to look at pictures of herself."

"May I look with you?" he asked.

"They're just family pictures. You'll probably get bored."

"No, I won't," he assured her. "I want to know everything there is to know about the Bradys."

When Shavonne returned an hour later, her arms filled with packages, she was astounded to find Slade, Megan, and Carrie Beth poring over the Brady family album.

She silently set down her packages. Her temples were pounding from the headache she'd awakened with. Not that she'd slept much last night. She'd tossed and turned for hours, thinking of Slade, of Quentin Ramsey's offer, of Slade, and Slade again.

When she'd finally fallen asleep Slade Ramsey had starred in her dreams too. She flushed at the memory. In one dream, he had been making love to her, kissing her, touching her, making her feel hot and wild. Little Courtney's cries had awakened her, abruptly ending the dream and leaving her aroused and unfulfilled. Her whole body had burned and ached, demanding the satisfaction it wasn't going to get. It was, she had fumed, a lousy way to start the day.

Battling the Saturday morning shopping crowds at the supermarket and discount department store hadn't helped her headache or her disposition. Erin and Courtney had come along, and the baby, fractious and teething, had howled the whole time. And now she'd finally arrived home, only to find Slade Ramsey cozily ensconced on her sofa, looking at family pictures with her sister and her niece.

She opened her mouth to order him out when Erin came into the house, balancing a bag of groceries on one hip and Courtney on the other. "Did Quentin Ramsey call yet?" Erin asked. Shavonne frantically motioned toward Slade in an attempt to alert her sister to his presence.

Her warning gesture was too late. Slade turned quickly and spied them standing in the doorway. Megan jumped up, her expression guilty. "No one called, Shavonne," she said nervously. "We—we didn't hear you come in. We were just looking at pictures."

Slade stood up as well. He was wearing well-fitting khaki chinos and a royal blue knit shirt with a little polo player on it, signifying brand name status. He looked crisp and virile and totally incongruous in their shabby, faded pink living room. His eyes met hers and she looked away, totally disconcerted and unable to hold his gaze.

"You were expecting a call from my father?" he asked.

"That's none of your business," she snapped. Her nerves were on edge, her head pounding. Now her stomach joined the fracas by lurching with anxiety.

She felt as shabby and faded as the living room in her pale pink skirt and pink and white blouse, neither of which possessed a brand name recognizable to anyone. She usually didn't concern herself with such things, but right now it didn't help her confidence one iota to have Slade looking so expensively elegant while she . . . didn't. Her clothes were cheap and looked it, and she knew it. And it bothered her that she was bothered by it. It was disturbing to realize that she wanted to look her best for Slade, that she was wishing she'd paused to comb her hair and apply fresh lipstick before entering the house. She lifted her hand to smooth her hair into place, then quickly dropped it, annoyed with herself.

She turned to her youngest sister. "Megan," she said irritably, "you know you're not supposed to let anyone into the house when you're here alone."

"Megan didn't let me in," Slade said. "I came in myself while she was tending to Carrie Beth. Now about this call from my father . . ."

"I'll give the children lunch and put the groceries away," Erin said quickly. "You can help me, Megan."

Slade forestalled them. "I told Megan and Carrie Beth that I'd take them into Morgantown to McDonald's for lunch. Then we're going shopping for Carrie Beth's birthday presents."

"I want a hamburger and a Pound Puppy," Carrie Beth said shyly. She had begun to warm up to Slade, although she wouldn't let him get too near her.

"Ohh!" Shavonne was incensed. "I knew you were conniving, Slade Ramsey, but I didn't think even you would resort to—to bribing children!"

"And I didn't think you would make deals with my father behind my back," he retorted. "It seems we both have things to learn about each other, Shavonne."

"I haven't made any deals with your father! He called me last night and made a very generous offer for Aunt Augusta's land. A far more generous offer than you made," she added pointedly.

"That land isn't Augusta's anymore, Shavonne, it's yours. And you're not selling it to anyone."

"Don't you think for one minute that you can tell

me what to do, Slade Ramsey!" She was enraged at his presumption. "When your father calls, I'm telling him that he can have the land for seventy-five thousand dollars."

"You could demand ten million dollars and you'd still be cheated out of its true worth," Slade said calmly.

"Ten million dollars?" Megan giggled. "Wow, that's carrying Mrs. Allen's supply and demand law kind of far."

"Don't pay a bit of attention to anything he says, Megan," Shavonne said, glowering at Slade. "He's just trying to trick us. Slade Ramsey is a lying, cheating, manipulative snake."

"Yes," he agreed with a nod. "I've been all those things and worse, Shavonne. But no longer. And my first redemptive act is going to be keeping your inheritance intact."

"But Shavonne doesn't want the land," Erin said, distressed, looking from Shavonne to Slade. "She wants the seventy-five thousand dollars."

"That land happens to have a one-hundred-million-dollar shopping mall built on it," he informed them. "And as owner of one-fourth of that property, in the eyes of the law Shavonne Brady is also entitled to one-fourth of its worth."

"No, that can't be," Megan argued. "That means Shavonne is entitled to twenty-five million dollars."

"Exactly." He nodded. "Needless to say, she won't be selling the land for a paltry seventy-five grand."

"I never thought I'd hear seventy-five thousand dollars referred to as paltry," Erin said rather dazedly.

"It's mere pocket change compared to the true value of the land," Slade said.

"This is absurd," Shavonne snapped. "Twenty-five million dollars—ha! If I were worth twenty-five million dollars, do you think Erin and I would've bought eneric paper plates and cups for Carrie Beth's birth-day party? Of course not. I would have gone into the Hallmark shop and bought an entire party set with their cutest design."

"You could buy the Hallmark shop itself with twenty-five million dollars," Megan said.

"There is no twenty-five million dollars, Megan. This is all part of some scheme he's concocted," Shavonne insisted. "And I want no part of whatever game you're playing, Slade Ramsey," she added sternly.

"Shavonne, I'm not playing games. I'm telling you the truth." He stared into her implacable dark eyes. How could he ever convince her? The economic gulf between them had never been more apparent than now. He was accustomed to dealing with seven- and eight-digit numbers; she couldn't comprehend them. He'd grown up taking for granted all the privileges of wealth, while her idea of great riches was being able to patronize card shops!

"Can we go to McDonald's now?" piped up Carrie Beth.

Shavonne glared at him. "I see you've reverted to type, Slade, making promises that you don't intend to keep. I won't let you use my family this way!"

"I'm not using anyone, Shavonne. And I intend to keep every promise I make. Taking the kids to lunch is one of the easier ones, both to make and to keep."

"No, it isn't. There's no way on God's green earth that I'll let you take my little sister and my little niece anywhere! I don't trust you out of my sight." She paused and gave a disdainful little sniff. "I don't trust you even when you're in plain view."

"No hamburger and no Pound Puppy?" Carrie Beth concluded regretfully.

"I think we'd better conduct this discussion alone,

Shavonne." His voice was terse. "We're upsetting Carrie Beth."

Shavonne fought a perilous urge to laugh aloud. This scene was bordering on the surrealistic. Slade Ramsey, the man with a self-proclaimed allergy to involvement and commitment, somehow had made himself sound like the wise and concerned father in a TV sitcom.

But she had no desire to upset her small niece, either. "All right, come into the kitchen," she said grudgingly. "But don't think you can make me change my mind about anything."

"Do you want Megan and me to take the kids outside, Shavonne?" Erin asked uncertainly.

"Yes, do that." Slade took the liberty of answering for Shavonne, then seized her hand in the most proprietary way to lead her into the kitchen.

Shavonne's temper flared. Slade Ramsey was a domineering man who wanted everything his own way, she reminded herself. He used people and manipulated their emotions, then walked away whenever it suited him. He'd done it to her once, but she wouldn't let him do it again. She wrenched her hand from his, picked up two bags of groceries, and stalked into the kitchen ahead of him.

Once there Slade faced her gravely. "Shavonne, I know you must—"

"You know nothing about me. Nothing at all! I'm no longer that nice little girl who lived and breathed to accommodate your every wish. I'm all grown up now and my first priority is protecting my family."

"And I admire you for it," he said swiftly. "I want to help you, Shavonne, I—"

"No thanks," she interrupted, scoffing. "We don't want or need any help from you!"

"I think you do, Shavonne." His voice was quiet and calm, in contrast to her emotional tones.

That only served to heighten her anger. "You're so smooth, so slick." She scowled at him. "You always were. Saying just what you knew I wanted to hear. The right words come easily to you, don't they, Slade? Too bad there isn't a shade of truth or meaning in any of them."

Slade stifled the flare of impatience that rocketed through him. Nice guys listen, he told himself. They don't simply overpower opposition. If he was to gain any credibility with Shavonne, he would have to revert to his old ways and allow her to change her mind about him on her own.

Shavonne paused, apparently waiting for him to bully her into refuting her allegations or to try to smooth-talk his way around her. When he said nothing at all, she became obviously disconcerted.

"You can't intimidate me," she said nervously, "or trick me into believing your lies. Honestly, Slade— twenty-five million dollars?" She gave a slight laugh of disbelief. "I know you think I'm hopelessly naive, but I can't believe you consider me birdbrained enough to swallow that sum!"

He tried to quell the frustration seething inside him. She had no reason to trust him, he reminded himself. On the contrary, she had every reason to distrust him.

He released a pent-up breath. Her dark eyes were flashing, her small chin set. Even in anger she was appealing, so vital and alive. Desire welled within him, a dangerous desire he didn't dare express. It was too soon. Shavonne would think he was trying to seduce her, that he intended to use her for a quick physical release. When in reality . . .

His heart thudded at the direction his thoughts were taking. He was finally beginning to realize why his life had seemed so empty—and why he had been unable to erase Shavonne from his mind. Guilt wasn't the only legacy of his affair with her. There was so much more.

He wanted her back! For the first time in two years, Slade faced the truth. He'd been a rat to walk out on her, but an even bigger fool to let her go.

His first impulse was to tell her so, right here, right now. But the timing for such an announcement was unbelievably bad. He cursed silently. Before he dared to make a move in winning her back, he had to deal with the pressing problem of that damn land! Determination surged through him. He *had* to get through to her.

"The whole situation must strike you as bizarre, not to mention suspicious," he said, almost conversationally. "First I arrive, totally unexpected, and offer you money for a piece of land you've never seen. And then my father calls that same night and triples my offer. Now, here I am telling you not to sell to my father and quoting a figure that strikes you as absurd. I don't blame you for being wary, Shavonne." To his own ears, he sounded like his reasonable, understanding old self.

He sounded reasonable and understanding to Shavonne, too. Totally unlike the cool, arrogant man she'd known. She stared at him, nonplussed. Was this yet another variation of his manipulative expertise? She didn't know what to make of him.

She searched his eyes for an answer. Her heart gave a queer little leap at the intensity she saw there. Was she imagining it? He was looking at her as if—as if— She gulped. As if he wanted her?

She felt her own immediate and involuntary response deep in the feminine core of her. An intensely sexual response. She remembered only too well just how good they'd been together in bed. The differences in their experience and background hadn't mattered there. They'd somehow been perfectly attuned to each other physically. Long after Slade had left her, she'd pondered how a cynical heartbreaker and a virginal innocent could have been so sexually well-matched . . .

But they had been. The passion between them had been honest and real. There had been no games, no manipulative power plays in bed. There they'd been in total accord, from the desire that flared hot and deep between them, to the sweet afterglow of mutual satisfaction.

"Shavonne?" Slade murmured. He was unable to drag his gaze from hers. Her brown eyes were cloudy and it reminded him . . . His body tightened and he grew hard at the erotic memory of Shavonne, moaning as she lay beneath him, her dark eyes slitted and unfocused as she neared her climax . . .

A flood of sensual memories washed over him. In his mind's eye, he saw himself lead Shavonne into his motel room, saw himself pull her into his arms and kiss her—a hot, deep kiss that she'd returned in full measure. He'd whisked her into bed within five days of their meeting, and they'd made love every day, sometimes twice, sometimes more, until he'd left her to return to Texas.

Her responses to him had been passionate and open and incredibly exciting. He'd been delighted to play teacher and she'd been an apt and eager student, enjoying the learning as much as he enjoyed the private tutoring. Their lovemaking, shattering in its intensity, had given them boundless pleasure, culminating in the bliss of mutual fulfillment. They had complemented each other perfectly, he remembered, as heat surged through him.

Was it possible that Shavonne was remembering too? His breath caught at the thought. He realized at that moment just how desperately he wanted her to want him again. Slowly, gently, he reached out to cup her cheek. His fingertips stroked her soft skin and desire jolted through him so forcefully, his body shook.

Just the touch of his hand on her cheek made her feel weak, Shavonne thought. A shaft of pleasure and need spun through her, and for a moment she feared her knees would buckle. She inhaled the heady masculine scent of him and it seemed to go straight to her head, affecting her like the most potent aphrodisiac.

Unconsciously, instinctively, they moved closer. Then the telephone rang, jarring them out of their enveloping sensual cocoon.

Four

Shavonne sprang away from Slade, her eyes widening in horror as she realized what had almost happened. She'd almost gone into his arms! Worse, she'd wanted to—and she had the sinking feeling he knew it. She winced as she turned to answer the phone. How could she be so weak, so foolish? She knew exactly what Slade Ramsey was, yet when he looked at her in that certain way, when he touched her . . . she wanted to go to him.

"Shavonne, let me answer the phone," he said urgently, as she reached for the receiver. He covered her hand with his own, preventing her from lifting the phone from its cradle. "If it's my father, I ought to be the one who talks to him."

Shavonne's heart was thundering in her chest. Lord, she thought. So that's why he'd done it? His smoldering, seductive gaze, his gentle caress which recalled—and promised—so much. She wanted to scream at her own naiveté. He'd deliberately cast his sexual spell over her in an attempt to bamboozle her into renouncing his father's offer for that damn land.

"I'll answer the phone," she said, and was infuriated by the trembling, breathless sound of her voice. "And I'll make my own decisions concerning my land!

47

Don't you dare try to drag me into whatever feud you have going with your father!"

She tried to push him away, to pick up the phone, but it was useless. Trying to move Slade was like trying to shove a two-ton boulder. She couldn't budge him an inch. He kept his hand firmly over hers, thus locking the receiver in place.

The phone continued to ring and Shavonne continued to try to answer it, but to no avail. Finally, the ringing stopped.

"Now see what you've done!" she said accusingly, furiously blinking back tears of rage. And frustration. And despair. Slade had proven once again how helpless she was against him, both physically and emotionally. But she was not going to surrender to him, she vowed fiercely. Not this time! He might have won this temporary battle, but she fully intended to win the war.

"I've saved you a fortune," he said quietly. "Trust me, Shavonne."

"I did, once. But never again!" She glared at him. "I'm finally beginning to understand what's going on here. Both you and your father want this land I've inherited from Aunt Augusta, and neither of you wants the other to get it. You thought you'd have the advantage because you knew me. That's why you came back—to get the land from me at a lower price than what your father intended to offer."

Slade groaned. "Sweetheart, you're way off-base."

"Don't try to sweet-talk me, you—you wheeling-dealing Ramsey! Why, Aunt Augusta was always telling us about her black-hearted kin. Plus, I have firsthand knowledge of what a rat you really are."

"Augusta was a Ramsey herself. She—"

"Exactly. She knew what she was talking about."

"Augusta Ramsey was hardly an unimpeachable source of information about the Ramsey family,

Shavonne. She carried on a feud with her own brother that lasted all their lives, for Pete's sake."

"I know." Shavonne nodded. "And in such a family, what could be more natural than for a father and a son to feud over money and property? And to try to beat out the other using whatever—or whoever—"

"Shavonne, you're twisting the facts to fit your own theory. Which happens to be one hundred percent wrong!"

"I don't think so, Slade." She shot him a triumphant little smile. "You can't believe it, can you? I've finally gotten wise to you. You thought you had only to offer what I'd consider to be a huge sum of money for the land and I'd jump to sell it."

"Which is exactly what you did," he reminded her grimly. "You couldn't wait to sign the bill of sale. If I were the unethical shark you accuse me of being, I'd have whipped out a contract yesterday and have the deed to that property in my possession right now."

She stared at him. That was true—or was it? There had to be an explanation as to why Slade hadn't proceeded with the sale of the land yesterday. He was right about one thing: dazzled by the twenty-five-thousand-dollar offer, she'd been ready and eager to sell.

The explanation she was looking for came to her suddenly. "Carrie Beth came out, and my sisters joined us a few minutes later. That's why you don't have the deed in your possession right now."

"Shavonne, I decided before anyone appeared that I wasn't going to buy the land from you at that unethically low price." Slade's desperation was growing. He'd done a masterful job of undermining her faith and trust in him. He understood her refusal to believe in him, yet was so damn frustrated that she didn't!

She turned away from him and began to remove

the groceries from the paper bags and set them on the counter. Clearly, for her the discussion was over.

It wasn't for Slade. "Dammit, Shavonne, why would I tell you about the shopping mall if I wanted to cheat you? Why would I tell you that your share is worth twenty-five million dollars when I could've bought it from you for twenty-five thousand?"

"I'm sure you had some devious reason, but I can't think what it is right now."

"I have every faith that you'll come up with something," he muttered gloomily.

She continued to unload the groceries. He picked up the margarine, the carton of eggs, and the gallon of milk and placed them in the refrigerator.

"What are you doing?" she asked.

"I'm helping you put away the groceries. Where do you keep your bread and cereal?"

She snatched the loaf of bread and the box of Cheerios away from him. "Go away! I'm busy and I don't want you hanging around here."

"Shall I take the kids to lunch then?"

His seemingly innocuous offer was made in the most polite and pleasant tone, but Shavonne froze at the sound of it. She knew how to read between the lines now. Slade was determined to get that land from her at his price, and he was subtly letting her know that he was prepared to use her family to achieve his aims.

She squared her shoulders. She couldn't allow that to happen, whatever the monetary cost. She may as well concede this round to Slade.

"All right!" she said jerkily. "You can have the land for twenty-five thousand dollars. When your father calls, I'll turn down his offer and tell him I'm selling to you instead."

"What?" Slade stared at her, perplexed. He'd asked to take the children to lunch and her response was *this*? "Shavonne—"

"I know, I know. You think I've lost my mind—not that you credit me with having much of a mind to begin with. I've just given up fifty thousand dollars by agreeing to sell you the land at the lower price." She swallowed. "But do you know what, Slade? It doesn't matter. Twenty-five, fifty, seventy-five thousand. None of those figures are real to me, anyway. They're all great sums and if one means getting rid of you faster, then I'll be satisfied with it."

He ran his hand through his hair, tousling it. He could never remember feeling so confused, so frustrated, and so maddened—all at the same time! "Shavonne, when you were a child, did you ever read that story about Alice, who went through the looking glass and found that what seemed familiar really wasn't? Well, I feel that way now, with you. I hear the words you're speaking, familiar words in plain English, yet what you're saying makes no sense to me."

"That's the way it is for me when it comes to men," she murmured, looking away from him. "A man says one thing and I hear another. Are they all deceptive or am I singularly stupid?"

A flash of jealousy seared him. "How many men have there been in your life, Shavonne?" he asked tightly, knowing he had no right to ask, expecting her to coldly tell him so, yet unable to prevent himself from voicing the question.

She paused and mentally counted. "Well, there's been you and my father and Erin's husband, Charlie Ray Tyler. And that's more than enough for me."

Slade knew that a sexually sophisticated woman would have detected his jealousy and used it as a weapon. A sexually sophisticated woman didn't count her father and brother-in-law as men in her life, didn't admit to having had just one lover. Her frank answer touched him.

"Megan told me about Tyler," he said softly. "I'm

well aware of my own abysmal conduct. What about your father, Shavonne? You've never mentioned him before."

"There isn't much to say about him." She shrugged uneasily. "He was just another man who said one thing and meant another. I can remember him telling me how much he loved my sisters and me. We were his little princesses, he said. And then he left, when Megan was just three months old. I was eight, and I remember the night he didn't come home as if it were yesterday. Mama was hysterical and I found the telegram he'd sent and read it. Daddy said that he'd gone to Ireland, that he didn't want to be married and didn't want to be a father. Later, Mama told me that he'd left the country because he didn't want to give us money for support. We haven't seen or heard from him since."

Slade drew in a sharp breath. Shavonne had been abandoned by her father? And then her lover had deserted her! "Shavonne . . ." he began achingly. If he'd felt like a cad before, he now felt on a par with Hitler.

She managed a wry little smile. "The Brady women haven't fared too well with the men in our lives. Maybe it's genetic."

His eyes captured hers. "Shavonne, my leaving Star City two years ago had nothing to do with you. I don't want you ever to feel that you were lacking in any way. You weren't. You were wonderful. Sweet and warm and loving. The problems were all with me."

"I had nothing to do with the fact that you didn't love me?" She laughed slightly. "Slade, I don't have *idiot* stamped on my forehead. Don't expect me to believe things that aren't true *this* time around."

She held his gaze steadily. He was the first to look away. "Two years ago you told me what you knew I wanted to hear," she continued. "You said that you oved me because you knew I never would have gone o bed with you otherwise. This time, let's stick with he truth."

Slade stared at the floor. "The truth is that you nad the misfortune of meeting me at a terrible, con-using time of my life. I was thirty-one years old and nad just been jilted by my fiancée—three weeks be-ore our wedding—because I wasn't the exciting, dangerous man of her fantasies. You've heard that old phrase 'nice guys finish last'? Well, I seemed to be living it, and I was sick and tired of it. I swore hat I would change myself and my image entirely. When I arrived in Star City shortly afterwards . . ."

"There I was," Shavonne finished slowly. "Kind of like a lab rat in an experiment. Available and able to test out the new you." A cold numbness settled over ner. According to Slade, he'd never even wanted her. Any woman would have done. Somehow, it was less painful and less humiliating to think of him as a genuine heartbreaker, a man incapable of commit-ment, who'd swept her off her feet only to drop her when she'd become serious about him.

But this . . . Her heart seemed to turn over. This new version of their affair robbed her of the last of her illusions—that she'd ever held any appeal for Slade. She was simply the first woman who had crossed his path after he'd decided to remake his image. She stared at him bleakly.

"Shavonne, I've spent the last two years and two months regretting the way I treated you," he said, his voice deep and low. He felt curiously light-hearted and realized that confessing and apologizing to Shavonne had lifted a crushing burden of guilt from him. It wasn't too late, he thought exultantly. He couldn't change the past, but he could reverse the consequences of it.

He gazed at Shavonne. She was beautiful. And sweet and loving and sexy. She had loved him passionately once. He was her first and only lover. There was no reason why they couldn't pick up the pieces of their past and build on it.

He felt as if he was on the verge of something profound and wonderful, something that would bring into his life the meaning that had been lacking. Two years ago, he'd been too blinded by bitterness to realize the value of what Shavonne had offered him. She'd promised warmth and love and happiness, and he had thrown it back in her face. But now . . .

"Everything is different now, Shavonne," he said as he moved toward her. "And this time—"

"This time?" she interrupted incredulously. "There isn't going to be any *this* time, Slade. I've never liked the story of Dr. Jekyll and Mr. Hyde, and finding out that I played a part in your own personal version of it *last* time has made me—"

"I know it sounds stupid and shallow," he said, grimacing. "And it was. *I* was. I was selfish and cruel. But not any longer, Shavonne. Sweetheart, I know that I have no right to ask but . . . can you, will you, forgive me?"

Shavonne heard the hopeful note in his voice, saw the expectant glimmer in his blue-gray eyes. He fully expected her to say yes, she thought. And then what?

Thinking that he'd used her solely for sex had been painful enough, but learning that he'd taken her love in a twisted plot of vengeance was even worse. She felt dehumanized. And angry. And not at all forgiving.

"I don't know if I want to forgive you," she said, her voice quavering. "You just told me that I meant nothing to you. That I was simply a stand-in for your ex-fiancée, taking her punishment because I happened to be at the wrong place at the wrong time. You were the man I loved and my first lover, but I didn't even exist as a person for you."

"Shavonne, that isn't true!" he protested.

"It's what you just told me." Her voice rose as her indignation mounted. *She hadn't even existed as a person for him!* "Are you changing your story again, Slade? Or your personality? Who or what do you plan to be this time around?"

The caustic edge to her voice both surprised and angered him. He hadn't expected sarcasm from Shavonne. Nor had he expected her to throw his apology back in his face. Ramseys seldom apologized. They were accustomed to the deferential treatment granted to the wealthy from birth, and apologies simply weren't part of their style. And Ramseys—even Slade, the nice one—didn't cope well when things didn't go their way. They weren't used to dealing with failure and frustration.

He'd humbled himself and asked for her forgiveness—and she wouldn't give it to him! Slade fumed. He'd decided that she was necessary for his happiness—and she'd opted out! His reaction was pure Ramsey.

"You know, something about this situation strikes me as familiar," he said harshly. "Here I am, being a nice guy, a humble penitent trying to make atonement, and what response does it bring from a woman? Scorn. Sarcasm. A drop-dead glare. Maybe women really do put nice guys and wimps in the same category. Last place!"

"I don't think you're a nice guy at all," Shavonne retorted crossly. "I think you're spoiled and egotistical. You think all you have to do is to say you're sorry and everything will be just the way you want it to be. Well, you're wrong, Slade. As far as I'm concerned, those are just more meaningless words from you."

"They aren't meaningless, dammit!"

Something seemed to explode inside him. Hearing her echo the conclusions he'd recently drawn about himself triggered a wild storm of emotions. Remorse and sorrow, shame, frustration, and confusion surged through him, becoming entangled and entwined with a hot burst of anger. His mind swirled. He couldn't think clearly, but he could react, and his instinctive reaction was all primitive male.

His hand snaked out and grabbed her wrist, jerking her toward him. Just as swiftly, his other arm went around her waist to bring her up against him. Before she could draw a breath or utter a word of protest, his mouth closed hotly over hers. He kissed her with an urgent, greedy hunger, his tongue thrusting deep, filling her with the taste of him.

Caught totally off-guard, Shavonne had no time to rally her defenses to counter his sensual assault. Her head spun wildly as she was overwhelmed by the touch and taste and feel of him. She hadn't been held, hadn't been kissed since he'd left her, and she was helpless to stop her body's traitorous responses to him.

She could feel his bold, obvious arousal as he held her tightly against his long, hard frame. One of his big hands massaged the base of her spine while the other caressed the nape of her neck with lazy erotic strokes. She shivered. She was exceptionally sensitive in both those places, and Slade knew it. He knew everything about her body, knew exactly where and how to touch her. He was the one who had awakened her to passion, he was the one who had taught her all about sexual excitement and arousal and fulfillment.

An insidious weakness crept through her and she went limp, her mind and body dissolving into eddies of dizzying delight.

A small ragged moan tore from her throat as she wrapped her arms around his neck, molding their bodies into a tantalizingly perfect fit. Her soft breasts impacted sensuously against the solid muscles of his chest. He thrust his thigh between hers, letting her feel the full force of his need, and she arched against him in instinctive feminine invitation, trying to soothe the almost unbearable ache deep inside her.

It had been so long and it felt so good to be in his arms. To hold him, to cling to him, to kiss him—deeply, hotly, urgently—the way he was kissing her. She felt as wild as the sensations shimmering inside her. She wanted to envelop him, to melt into him . . . She knew how it would be. The exquisite pleasure building into a sublime tension, their bodies merging with fevered anticipation, the glorious abandon as they moved together, the white-hot readiness exploding in spasms of ecstasy.

She had missed him so much. She wanted this, *needed* it. She needed him . . .

"What are you doing?"

The shrill, somewhat accusatory voice ripped through the haze of passion enveloping them. Shavonne and Slade automatically sprang apart, their faces flushed and their eyes glazed. Both stared somewhat dazedly down at Carrie Beth. The little girl was eyeing them with a mixture of curiosity and suspicion.

Slade was the first to recover his wits. "What are we doing?" he repeated with a low chuckle. He reached for Shavonne and hauled her against him, using both arms to secure her in front of him. "We had a little fight and now we're kissing and making up."

Shavonne blushed scarlet and tried to wriggle out of his grasp. Her legs felt shaky and her whole body was throbbing with the unslaked desire Slade had so effortlessly evoked in her. Would he have this seemingly irresistible sexual power over her forever? she wondered, thoroughly unsettled by her intense response to him. Even now, her body was reacting to his nearness. It took great willpower to resist lean-

ing into his warm strength and relaxing against
him.

His lips brushed the top of her head, and his
warm breath rustled her hair as he spoke. "And
now we're *all* going to lunch together, aren't we,
Shavonne?"

"We're not going anywhere!" she said through
clenched teeth, fighting the urge to wrestle her way
out of his arms. She didn't dare expose her nervous
niece to a full-scale adult scuffle. "Let me go, Slade."
It was hard to sound calm when she was so disgusted with herself. She had fallen into his hands
like a ripe peach!

"Not until you say you'll have lunch with Carrie
Beth and me," he said lightly.

She blew out an angry breath. "It's not going to
work, Slade. You're not going to charm, bully, or
manipulate me into doing what you want."

"Suppose I simply ask you?" he replied quietly.
"Please come with me, Shavonne."

How did one deal with a reasonable request, devoid of threat or manipulation? With a reasonable
refusal, Shavonne decided. "We can't go to lunch,"
she said tightly, standing tense and rigid in his
hold. "I have a million things to do today. There are
ten children arriving at three-thirty this afternoon
for Carrie Beth's birthday party, and Erin and I have
to bake the cake and blow up two dozen balloons
and—"

"We have plenty of time," Slade said. "I promise everything will get done." He held her closer,
inhaling the clean fragrance of her hair and savoring the softness of her feminine curves pressed tightly
against him. "We all have to eat, don't we? Say you'll
come, Shavonne."

He thought of her instantaneous and incandescent response when he'd kissed her, and heat flamed
through him. She was hurt and angry, but she had

esponded passionately to him. She might be fighting him on one level, but on a primitive, physical level, she still wanted him. The realization elated him.

He would build on that, he promised himself. And once a Ramsey decided on a course of action, it was no holds barred until the goal was achieved. He nuzzled her neck as he lightly stroked her stomach.

Shavonne's legs felt weak. The sensual kneading of his hands sent flames of liquid fire licking through her veins. She could feel her self-control wavering. She wanted . . . she needed . . . She drew in a sharp, painful breath. She *had* to get away from him!

"All right, we'll all go to lunch with you, providing you let me go this instant!" she said, as she tried to pry his arms loose.

"Whatever you say, sweetheart." He dropped a quick kiss on her nape and released her.

She quickly stepped away from him, shooting him a baleful glare. Her neck was still tingling from the touch of his lips, and the feel of his hard frame seemed to be imprinted on the length of her body.

"Let's go," he said with all the hearty enthusiasm of a Scout leader rounding up his troops. He extended a hand to Carrie Beth.

Carrie Beth looked at him with huge brown eyes and did not take his hand. "Shavonne going?" she asked apprehensively. "Mommy going?"

"Yes, everyone's going," Slade jovially assured her. "Your mommy, Shavonne, Courtney, Megan—and Colleen and Tara, too. Hey, where are Colleen and Tara, anyway?"

"They're at work," Shavonne said shortly. "They both have part-time jobs at the Mountaineer Mall. And since when do you know all my sisters' names? You never did before."

"Since I looked at the photo album this morning. I learned a lot about you and the Bradys, Shavonne.

But not enough. I want to know everything there is to know about you." His voice deepened with emotion.

She ignored him. She couldn't cope with him any other way. She felt as if she were caught in an emotional whirlpool, buffeted by conflicting feelings.

The way he was looking at her now was almost as arousing as his touch. Rather desperately, she scooped up Carrie Beth and headed outside. He followed her, gripping her elbow to steady her when she stumbled slightly.

She reacted even to that brief, non-sexual touch. Her body throbbed and tingled sensuously, expectantly. She was furious with herself and her wanton responses. She whirled away from him, glowering. "If we're going, then we'd better leave now. I want to get this ordeal over with as soon as possible."

Five

"I've never spent a day like this one," Shavonne said to Erin as she and her sister served ice cream and cake to twelve excited toddlers. Most of the little party guests' mothers were present, too, and Megan was serving the adults. The noise level was incredible, but it wasn't the noise that was disconcerting Shavonne.

"None of us have ever spent a day like this one," Erin muttered. "Today has been like—like something out of *Lifestyles of the Rich and Famous*."

"Carrie Beth, Courtney, look at me and smile," Slade instructed from across the room. "Okay, the rest of you kids run through the Happy Birthday song one more time. Ready . . . lead them into it, Megan."

Slade was recording the event with the audio/video camera he had purchased at the mall earlier in the day. The tape could be instantly played on the videocassette recorder that he'd bought at the same time. He'd also bought a wide screen color television set to go with the VCR. He'd been incredulous that the Bradys owned only one television set, and a black and white one, at that! He had immediately set out to remedy their plight.

"Shavonne," he called, and she looked up. "Smile,

honey, you're on camera." Later, on the videotape, she would appear dazed. Which she was, Shavonne was the first to admit. She'd been in a daze since Slade had taken them to lunch.

When they'd all gone to McDonald's, she had sardonically remarked that one meal with two young children would be all Slade Ramsey could tolerate. He wouldn't be able to hustle the Bradys back home fast enough!

But it hadn't worked out that way. Slade had seemed to enjoy himself thoroughly. He was unfazed by ketchup smeared on little faces and fingers, by the inevitable spilled drinks, by the pieces of hamburger and bun and french fries littering the floor under their table.

When the meal was over, he hadn't pleaded to be relieved of their company. He had suggested that they all go to the mall and pay a visit to Colleen and Tara, who were working as salesclerks in two of the shops there.

What followed left Shavonne and her sisters too stunned to protest, too awed to do anything but stand by and stare as Slade Ramsey launched a shopping spree the likes of which the Mountaineer Mall had never seen.

He'd taken Courtney and Carrie Beth into a toy store first and had proceeded to strip the shelves of anything and everything the children happened to glance at. Dolls, stuffed animals, blocks, tea sets. He had seemed as delighted to pay for the toys as the children were to select them. Next he had swept the girls into a children's clothing shop, one in which the Bradys window-shopped only, due to the high prices of the exclusive merchandise.

The prices hadn't deterred Slade. In fact, he hadn't even glanced at the price tags. Play clothes, pajamas, the frilliest party dresses for Carrie Beth and Courtney—he had insisted on buying them all.

Shavonne stared at the children who were glee-fully shoveling cake and ice cream into—and onto—themselves as they sat around the decorated table. Her nieces were wearing exquisite hand-embroidered dresses of baby pink and looked like two small blond princesses. Both wore dress shoes that were ridiculously impractical and exorbitantly expensive.

Carrie Beth was particularly thrilled with her new shoes. She showed them to everyone and kept glancing down at them, her big brown eyes glowing with pride. Shavonne's own eyes blurred with tears. Slade was giving her family things they could never have had, and though she distrusted his unexpected display of generosity, she couldn't begrudge her family's enjoyment of it.

What *were* his motives? she wondered as she continued to review mentally the incredible day at the mall.

After purchasing the children's things and the camera and video equipment, Slade had announced that he planned to outfit the Brady sisters. Shavonne had quickly refused his offer and Erin had followed her lead. Not Megan, though. Caught up in the excitement, the youngest Brady sister had been willing and eager to let Slade buy her the clothes she'd always dreamed of.

Shavonne said no, but she'd been saying no all afternoon. Slade either never heard her or was deliberately ignoring her. He waltzed Megan into a shop specializing in clothes for teenage girls and told her to choose whatever she wanted for herself, Colleen, and Tara. Megan didn't hesitate to obey.

Later, on their way to the car, Shavonne managed to maneuver Slade to the back of the group. "I don't understand, Slade. Why are you doing this?" she asked, wary and genuinely baffled by his largess.

He smiled. "Because I want to. I usually hate to shop, but I can't remember when I've had a better time at a mall. And this one is less than half the size of the Ramsey malls."

"Ramsey *malls*?" she echoed uncertainly.

"We've built shopping malls and office complexes all over the country. The Ramsey Park Mall, of which you're part-owner, is just one of them."

She ignored his reference to the mall she allegedly owned a part of. Shavonne Brady, mall-mogul. It was too ludicrous to rate a response!

But she had no trouble believing that Slade Ramsey owned malls—and heaven only knew what else. "You're rich," she said softly. It was a revelation to her, and she cast him a covert glance. She'd never known anyone who was rich. Hadn't she read that "the rich are different from you and me"? She'd always believed it.

She swallowed. "I—I didn't know. Until today, that is."

His smile faded. "No, I never spent much money on you last time, did I?" He'd taken her to drive-in movies and drive-in restaurants—and his motel room. Not much of a courtship, he thought regretfully. "But *this* time . . ."

"I don't want you to spend anything on me," she said fiercely. She might be poor, but she wasn't for sale.

"You've made that quite clear. You wouldn't let me buy you a thing today. And I want to, Shavonne. I want to give you everything that you—"

"There are names for women who let rich men give them things!" Did allowing her family to accept Slade's gifts make her one of them?

"You'll never fall into that category, sweetheart," he said quickly. "I enjoyed getting these things for the kids. Making them happy has made me happier than I've been in a long time."

She stalked away from him, shaking. It was hard to be on guard against someone who took pleasure in her family's happiness. It was hard not to like someone who had so generously and warmly showered her sisters and nieces with wonderful gifts. And most of all, it was hard to remain cool and aloof toward the man who had once been her lover, and who still possessed the power to ignite her passion.

Slade had to make three trips back and forth to the mall to get all his passengers and packages home, but he didn't utter a single complaint. And after his final trip, he'd arrived with a bakery sheet cake, dozens of helium-inflated balloons, and an entire Hallmark party ensemble with a cute teddy bear design.

"Now you don't have to bake or blow up balloons," he had said, smiling at Shavonne in a way that had made her feel light-headed. "And you can ax the generic plates and cups."

"You're like Santa Claus and a fairy godfather all rolled up into one," a dazzled Megan had told him.

"It's my pleasure, honey," he had said, positively beaming with delight. Shavonne and Erin had exchanged nervous glances. Neither was as trusting or as easily impressed as their little sister.

"He's spent a fortune on the family today," Erin now whispered to Shavonne, as they watched Carrie Beth gleefully rip through the pile of brightly wrapped gifts. "Can he want the land that much?" Erin obviously had drawn her own conclusions concerning Slade's generosity. "Maybe it really is worth more than seventy-five thousand dollars."

"Sure it is, Erin. It's worth twenty-five million, remember?" Shavonne replied cheekily. For reasons she didn't quite understand, she didn't tell her sister that she'd already offered to sell Slade the land at the price he'd originally offered.

"Twenty-five million!" Erin grinned at the outlandish figure. "Don't you wish we could've heard Aunt Augusta's reaction to that one?"

"She would have given us dire warnings about sneaky, lying, double-crossing Harlan's sneaky, lying, double-crossing grandson."

"I wonder what started Aunt Augusta's feud with her brother Harlan?" Erin mused idly. "She never would say."

"She carried that secret to her grave," Shavonne said, watching Slade film Carrie Beth's excited response to a new doll. "Along with her feud with Harlan and his kin."

"The Ramseys are a strange breed," Erin said with a shrug. "Shavonne, I know that I'm certainly not qualified ever to give advice about men to anyone, but be careful around Slade Ramsey. I remember how badly he hurt you the last time."

Shavonne murmured an inarticulate response. She thought of her conversation with Slade in the kitchen that morning, when he had tried to explain why he'd so heartlessly ended their affair two years ago.

His voice had seemed to hold genuine regret; his gray-blue eyes had seemed to mirror his pain. *Seemed.* That was the word that kept tripping her up. During their affair, he'd spent so much time with her, he'd made love to her so often and so passionately, that it had *seemed* as if he loved her. He'd even said he did.

And she'd believed it, but it hadn't been true. Now he was trying to convince her that he was really a nice guy who'd merely been pretending to be a smooth-talking heartbreaker. He was also trying to convince her that she was an heiress, worth millions of dollars.

She groaned inwardly. She'd never been so confused in her life. The only certainty she could derive from the situation was that nothing was as it seemed.

The sisters were standing on the porch, bidding good-bye to the last of the party guests, when Megan tapped Shavonne's shoulder and whispered, "It's him, Shavonne. Quentin Ramsey is on the phone."

Shavonne's eyes flew to Slade, who was filming Carrie Beth and Courtney frolicking in the front yard. Without a word she slipped inside to take the call.

"Well, Miss Brady!" Quentin greeted her heartily. "How's that son of mine behaving?"

You wouldn't believe me if I told you, was Shavonne's silent reply. However, she simply said, in the most noncommital voice she could muster, "We've discussed the sale of the land."

"Ah, yes, yes. The land," Quentin said, as if the subject had just occurred to him. "I assume you told Slade about the offer I made last night."

"Oh, yes, I told him." Shavonne swallowed hard. Her palms were growing damp. She was as unfamiliar with games of financial intrigue as she'd been with games between the sexes. She took a deep breath and plunged ahead. "Mr. Ramsey, Slade told me that the property your Aunt Augusta left me is worth twenty-five million dollars."

There was a half-second's pause. Then Quentin said incredulously, "He *told* you that?"

Shavonne winced. She'd done it again, she'd made a total fool of herself. She'd now bombed in both romance and finance. "Naturally, I didn't believe him for a moment," she said quickly.

"You didn't believe him?" Quentin repeated carefully.

"No, Mr. Ramsey. Did you actually think that I would?" He probably did, she thought glumly. Heaven only knew what Slade had told his father about her. Her face burned.

"Well." Quentin audibly cleared his throat. "I'm beginning to see things in a whole new perspective." Shavonne was certain that she heard respect in his tone, and her humiliation eased somewhat.

The ball was in her court, and she played it gamely. "Mr. Ramsey, you probably won't understand why I'm going to do this, but—" She paused, taking time out to breathe. "I told Slade that I would sell him the land at the price he offered me. Twenty-five thousand dollars."

There was a full minute of silence on the other end of the line. And then, hesitantly, Quentin asked, "Miss Brady, are you jesting?"

"No, I'm not, Mr. Ramsey. But I'm going to sell the land to Slade only on one condition—that he make the first move to patch up the feud that you and he are carrying on."

"The feud?"

"Oh, Slade didn't tell me about it, but it wasn't too hard to figure out, with the two of you bidding on the land and all. And, of course, having lived next door to Aunt Augusta all my life, I know how partial you Ramseys are to feuds. I always thought it was so sad that she was alienated from her own blood kin all those years, and that she died without ever making up with them."

"And so to spare Slade and me from making a similar mistake, you're willing to sell him the land—"

"Because he asked me first," she put in quickly, "and only if he—"

"Promises not to extend our . . . feud. Well, Miss Brady, I must admit you've caught me off-guard, something that seldom happens. You're a very . . . unusual young woman, to say the least."

"It's just that I believe in family, Mr. Ramsey. And it's . . . well, it's only right that Augusta Ramsey's land should end the feud between you and your son. Sort of a way of finally laying to rest her own feud with her brother Harlan after all these years." Shavonne smiled. Her decision warmed her. She knew she was doing the right thing.

"Miss Brady," Quentin began. There was a long

pause, then he spoke again. "Miss Brady, I'm about to make an extraordinary proposal, but then, it's only fitting that I do, as your actions are indeed . . . er, extraordinary. I'd like to send you a cashier's check for fifty thousand dollars, the amount of money that you are so unselfishly willing to give up in order to restore peace in the Ramsey family. Would you accept my check, Miss Brady?"

"Oh, Mr. Ramsey!" She was stunned. "I'm overwhelmed. I—I never expected this!"

"I want you to take the money, Miss Brady. I insist upon it."

"Mr. Ramsey, you're a fine, generous man." She blinked back the hot tears that filled her eyes. "I'm only sorry that your Aunt Augusta missed the opportunity to know you."

"Perhaps she's looking down on us from somewhere in the Great Beyond, Miss Brady," Quentin said dryly, "and I can just imagine what she's thinking."

He paused briefly, then continued, "It's been a pleasure doing business with you, Miss Brady. You'll have my check—and my son's—as soon as you sign the contract that our attorneys will draft immediately. A representative of our firm will fly to West Virginia in the morning with the papers, and the business will be transacted right there in Star City. If that meets with your approval, of course," he added deferentially.

He was such a gentleman, Shavonne thought warmly. "Yes, that will be fine, Mr. Ramsey." Tomorrow morning, she and her sisters would have seventy-five thousand dollars! She was elated. "Good-bye, Mr. Ramsey. It was a pleasure doing business with you, too!"

She hung up the phone and raced outside. Colleen had just arrived home from her job at the mall, and was standing on the porch talking to Erin,

Megan, and Slade. The two little girls were playing in the front yard. "Where's Tara?" Shavonne asked excitedly. "I'd like everybody to hear the good news."

"Tara agreed to work late, till nine tonight," Colleen said. "What's the good news, Shavonne? Please don't make us wait until Tara comes home!"

Slade stared at Shavonne and felt his body tighten with desire. Her cheeks were flushed and her beautiful eyes were glowing. He remembered the way her face used to light up at the sight of him, her cheeks pink and eyes shining, just as they were now. Except this time, her delight had nothing to do with his presence, he reminded himself sadly.

"What's your good news, honey?" he asked, and felt a wrench when she turned to him. She pulled her face into an expressionless mask and her dark eyes cooled.

"I just spoke to your father," she said briskly, "and I told him that I'd agreed to sell the land to you for your original offer of twenty-five thousand dollars. On the condition that—"

"You *what*?" he roared. "Shavonne, you have no idea what you've done! He'll have one of his attorneys fly up here tonight and—"

"Tomorrow," she corrected him coolly. "The attorney is flying up tomorrow with the papers to sign and—" She turned to her sisters, and the excitement was back in her eyes. "Quentin Ramsey insisted that I accept a check for fifty thousand dollars from him, even though I agreed to sell the land to Slade for twenty-five."

Colleen and Megan screamed with joy and jumped up and down, hugging each other. Erin threw her arms around Shavonne. Carrie Beth and Courtney, seeing the commotion, began to shriek and hug each other in raucous imitation.

Slade watched the scene and felt sick. He cursed his father and he cursed his Great-Aunt Augusta. So this was the stuff that life-long feuds were founded upon. He knew he couldn't stand by and watch Shavonne and her family be cheated out of what was rightfully theirs. And he knew his father and brothers would never forgive him for interfering in what promised to be Ramsey & Sons' greatest financial coup ever—paying just seventy-five thousand dollars for a twenty-five-million-dollar property.

"You're not going to sign anything until you've seen the property you've inherited, Shavonne," he said firmly, his voice loud enough to be heard over the joyful racket.

Shavonne swung around to face him. "The game is over, Slade. I'm signing those papers in the morning."

"And I'll have an attorney present to keep you from doing it."

"You can't do that!" she cried.

"Oh, yes, I can. And I will." Slade wished he was as sure as he sounded. He hoped that he wouldn't have to put his bluff into operation. Just the thought of explaining this situation to any lawyer gave him a chill.

"I can sell my land to whoever I want to!" Shavonne said. "It's all perfectly legal. There's nothing you or any lawyer can do to stop me."

"I can certainly stop you since you're planning to sell the land to me. I refuse to buy it until you've seen it. And don't think you can turn around and sell it to my father," he said, "or I'll slap you with a—a *res judicata* so fast your head will spin."

He watched her certainty fade and was grateful that he knew a few Latin legal terms to throw around, though this particular one had nothing to do with the buying and selling of land. It sounded intimidatingly official, though. He watched Shavonne turn unhappily to her sisters and resisted the urge to snatch her into his arms. He knew she wouldn't let him touch her, not while she viewed him as an obstacle to her and her sisters' dreams of solvency.

"Slade, why won't you buy the land?" Megan asked plaintively. "We really need that money. We can pay off all our bills and not have to worry about having our electricity or gas or telephone shut off again."

Slade clenched his jaw. "Megan, I promise that you'll never have to worry about paying the utility bills—or any bills—again." Dammit, his father should have to hear this, he thought. A young girl Megan's age should be enjoying school and parties and clothes, like his sister Vanessa had, not worrying about her family's ability to pay the utility bills!

"Megan, don't ask that man for any favors," Shavonne said angrily. "I—"

"You're leaving for Houston with me tonight," he interrupted, "and I'm not taking no for an answer, Shavonne. I'll take you to Texas, even if I have to rent a private jet and carry you aboard bound and gagged."

"You wouldn't dare!" she said breathlessly.

"Ramseys are notorious for taking dares, Shavonne, so I'd advise you not to issue them." He took a step toward her.

"Shavonne, what are we going to do?" Colleen squeaked, clutching Shavonne's arm.

Slade was astonished by the terror on the girl's face. Even Megan, his ally, had moved behind a wide-eyed Erin and was watching him anxiously. Then he remembered that the Bradys' dealings with males, aside from their erstwhile father, was limited to the late Charlie Ray Tyler, the man who had engaged in activities like breaking arms and threatening little children.

Slade was chagrinned to be classed in such company. His gaze moved to Shavonne, who was standing slightly in front of her three younger sisters, her

fists clenched tightly, her face tense. She was fighting it, but he knew she was frightened, too.

"I didn't mean to sound threatening," he said hastily to assure them, and groaned silently. It was ironic
that they'd cast him in the role of terrifying tyrant
when all he was trying to do was to preserve the
fortune they didn't believe they had. "I want all of
you to come to Texas," he heard himself say. At this
point, he knew he would say anything to erase the
fear from the four pairs of dark velvet eyes.

"I mean it," he went on eagerly. "Shavonne, I'd
like you and your sisters and the two babies to fly to
Houston with me tonight. We'll see your property
and find you a lawyer. You're definitely going to
need legal representation to protect your financial
interests."

Megan sighed with relief. "You looked so mad,
Slade! I was sure you were going to start beating up
on Shavonne."

"Not all men resort to violence," he said quietly.
"Or desertion." His eyes met Shavonne's. "Please,
Shavonne. Come with me. I know I don't deserve
your trust, but I'm asking you to please trust me in
this one matter anyway."

Shavonne looked away. All her instincts were urging her to trust Slade. Then again, the last time
she'd followed her instincts and given in to her love
for him, she'd been burned. But there was a differ-
ence now, she silently argued with herself. This time
she wasn't in love with Slade. This time he couldn't
hurt her, not even financially, because she always
had Quentin Ramsey's offer to fall back on should
Slade refuse to buy the land.

"Do you really want all of us to go to Houston with
you?" Colleen asked Slade, her expression brighten-
ing. "We've never flown before," she added breathlessly. "We've never been out of West Virginia before."

"We've never been anywhere but Morgantown,"

Megan added. "Shavonne, can we please, please go to Texas?"

"But what about school?" she asked. "And Tara's classes at the university?"

"Lots of kids in our high school get excused to take trips with their families," Colleen said quickly. "Megan and I can make up the work. And so can Tara."

"And what will we do about our day nursery?" asked Erin, who appeared to share Shavonne's reluctance to leave. "Those mothers depend on us to keep their kids during the weekdays—and we depend on their money for doing it."

"Call the mothers tonight," Slade said, "and tell them to make other temporary arrangements for their children because you're taking a vacation. You're entitled to some time off," he added before Shavonne or Erin could issue another protest. "Now, why don't all of you go inside and start packing?"

"We don't have any suitcases," Colleen said. "I guess we can't put our stuff in laundry bags, huh?"

"Carry laundry bags onto the airplane?" Megan was aghast. "Colleen Brady, we'd look like something out of the *Beverly Hillbillies!*"

"You don't have any suitcases?" Slade asked. He could scarcely comprehend it. "Not even one?" He took things such as suitcases for granted, as essential and available as towels and dishes and the like. One went to the proper place and there they were, ready for use.

Shavonne shattered his illusion. "We never go anywhere, so why should we waste money on a suitcase? And we—"

"—are going right now to buy one," he interrupted. He could see her using the lack of a suitcase as a reason against making the trip to Houston. "Come on, honey. We'll go back to the mall, buy some suitcases, and then give Tara a ride home. No need for her to take the bus, when we'll be right there to give her a lift, hmm?"

He was aware that he was talking too much and too fast, but what alternative did he have? he asked himself as he took Shavonne's hand and half-dragged her down the porch steps. Perhaps it wasn't fair to overwhelm her this way, but he would make it up to her. When they got to Texas and the issue of her land had been fairly dealt with, then he would woo her slowly and romantically. He would try to win back her trust and her love. But until then . . .

He heaved a heavy sigh. His first priority was making sure that his father didn't steal her land. He would have to use whatever methods he could to insure her financial protection.

"Wanna go to the mall with that daddy!" howled Carrie Beth. She'd asked where Slade and Shavonne were going and been informed that she wasn't invited along.

"I'm flattered that she wants to go with me," Slade said as he patted Carrie Beth's head. The little girl was hanging on to his leg, shrieking her demand to be included in the outing. "Earlier today, she wouldn't take my hand or let me touch her."

"No wonder she wants to go with you," Shavonne said wryly as she watched her niece wail. "You practically bought her the mall the last time you were there."

"She called me Daddy," he said musingly.

"Small *d*," Shavonne said dampeningly. "Carrie Beth and Courtney call all men daddy. It's a generic term they use interchangeably with man." She pried her small niece loose from Slade and ordered her into the house.

Carrie Beth stuck out her lower lip in a pout. "Mad at you, Shavonne," she said crossly, and stomped away in high dudgeon.

Shavonne shook her head and rolled her eyes heavenward. "It looks like you've made a conquest," she said in a tone that clearly questioned the little girl's judgment. "And they say you can't buy love!"

Slade's lips curved into a mirthless smile. "You don't want to believe that I'm a man a child could like, that I'm a man who genuinely likes kids."

Shavonne remembered the lost child in the supermarket two years ago, and thought of how natural he'd been with Carrie Beth and Courtney today. But was it real or had he been acting? And how was she supposed to know? She'd better find out for she was in danger of liking this new Slade Ramsey, she warned herself grimly.

She walked swiftly to his rented car, but he arrived there first, in time to open the door for her and assist her inside. His gentlemanly courtesy warmed her; she wasn't used to such attentions. Oh, she was in grave danger of liking him. Way too much.

"I'm wondering who you're trying to be in your current incarnation here in Star City," she said in a deliberate attempt to antagonize him. It would be easier not to like him if he was furious with her. "Mr. Rogers? Or a game show host, showering prizes on today's lucky contestants? I've seen elements of both in you today."

He gripped the wheel tightly as he steered the car along the winding rural road. "You've been hurt, Shavonne. I can understand why you feel the need to attack me."

"And now you're the understanding analyst, explaining and accepting feminine hostility," she taunted, determined to provoke him.

"Shavonne," he said in a carefully patient voice, "I just want you to know that you're safe with me, that I'm not going to hurt you or use you."

"Ah, he slips effortlessly into the role of Sir Galahad. Very impressive. I dare anyone to identify the *real* Slade Ramsey, whoever he might be."

He glanced at her and caught her sneaking a covert look at him. His brows pulled together and he frowned thoughtfully. "Correct me if I'm wrong, but is it possible that there's an element of sexual provocation in these jibes you keep tossing at me?"

"Oh!" She was immediately and completely incensed. "You're wrong, all right! You're totally wrong! Mister, you couldn't be more wrong if you—"

"I get your point," he interrupted dryly. "I'm wrong. No need to bludgeon me over the head with it."

But Shavonne wasn't about to let it drop. "Sexual provocation? Me? Sexually provoking you? Not a chance, Ramsey. Only an arrogant blockhead like you would even think such a thing, let alone have the gall to say it!"

He shrugged. "Just asking. No need for a character assassination, Shavonne."

"I haven't even begun to assassinate your character—or the lack of it!"

"Well, by all means, proceed. You must have some great ammunition stored up."

"You're laughing at me!" For the first time in her life, Shavonne actually experienced the colorful sensation of seeing red. Fury surged through her as sparkling red lights danced before her eyes, blinding her to everything but the powerful drive to fight. "You're just like your grandfather Harlan Ramsey, an underhanded, vain—"

"Sounds like a direct quote from Great-Aunt Augusta. Don't forget the 'he lived and breathed to do the devil's work' part of it."

Shavonne was so involved in her outrage that she failed to notice that Slade had pulled the car off the road and parked it on the shoulder. That he had shut off the engine, and they were sitting alone in the silent, deserted darkness.

He turned to her. "Surely you can come up with something more original than a secondhand rehash of Augusta and Harlan's old feud. Isn't there anything personal you'd like to add?" She didn't miss the mocking note in his voice, and it sent her rage higher. She shook with the force of her emotions bubbling through her. She wanted to lash out at him, both verbally and physically, to scream insults at him and slap him with all her strength. It was the prospect of herself resorting to violence that shocked her out of the insanity consuming her.

All she could think of was Erin's loathsome husband and his terrifying lack of control when he was angered. Never, never would she allow herself to be driven to his level of animalistic behavior.

She closed her eyes and sat back in the seat, breathing deeply as she attempted to calm herself.

"Aren't you going to revile me as a ruthless, selfish cad," Slade asked, "who plied you with champagne and then took your virginity when you were too tipsy to know what you were doing?"

A charge of sexual electricity jolted through her. That day was indelibly stamped in her memory. They'd had a picnic at Cheat Lake with champagne and a whole basket of gourmet delicacies that Slade had bought for the occasion. It was the first time she'd ever sampled any of them, including the champagne. She remembered the warm, floating feeling she'd had after her third glass. She remembered the desire that had coursed through her when Slade had taken her in his arms, when his mouth had opened over hers. She remembered the thrust of his tongue, the wildness she'd felt when his hands touched her breasts . . .

Shavonne's breath caught in her throat. The sensual memories of that day managed to evoke startlingly similar feelings tonight. A syrupy warmth flowed sweetly through her.

"Of course," he continued softly, "if you're set on a character assassination, you won't admit the truth about that day, Shavonne. You won't admit that although you might have had a little too much to drink, you were completely aware of what you were doing. You wanted me as much as I wanted you."

He leaned toward her, his gray eyes glittering with . . .

Passion! She stared at him. Even in the darkness, she could see that his face was flushed, his breathing was erratic. He wasn't angry; he was as aroused as she by the powerfully evocative memories. And he was right, she acknowledged dreamily. She had known what she was doing that day. She'd never claimed otherwise.

"You're deliberately goading me," she said breathlessly.

"It's called sexual provocation. Just what you were doing earlier."

"No!"

"You didn't want to fight with me, Shavonne? You didn't want our quarrel to end this way?" With lightning speed, his fingers fastened around her wrists. Their gazes locked as he slowly, purposefully, drew her toward him.

Six

They continued to stare into each other's eyes as Slade gently pushed Shavonne against the back of the cushioned seat. He settled himself against her, letting her feel the weight and hardness of his body. His arms tightened around her, and she felt surrounded by him, caught in his sensual, masculine trap.

"Sexual provocation," she murmured huskily. "Is this where it leads?"

"Right where we both want to be." His eyes burned into hers. "I've been aching to touch you, Shavonne. To hold you, to have you to myself."

She should be fighting him off, Shavonne reminded herself. She ought to be plotting to extricate herself from this undeniably sexually provocative position. She tried to summon the anger that had driven her earlier but, curiously, her rage had been diffused, leaving her languid and limp. Instead of trying to fight or escape, her arms stole around his neck and she relaxed against his warmth and strength with a soft sigh.

He was right, she thought achingly. Heaven help her, she was where she wanted to be. Would it be foolish or risky if she stayed here, for just a few minutes? She sighed again. It was probably both, but it felt so right to be back in his arms.

"Remember the first time I held you this way?" he asked, nuzzling her neck. "You looked at me with those big dark velvet eyes of yours and said, 'I've never been this close to a man before.' My head swam. I couldn't believe the potent effect you had on me. That you still have on me, Shavonne."

She felt a rush of intoxicating excitement and steeled herself against it. "I—I shouldn't let you—"

He silenced her by tracing her lips with two long fingers. "You said that the first time, too. You didn't mean it then, and you don't mean it now. You want me, Shavonne. Just as much as I want you."

She stared at him with wide eyes. Two years ago she had loved this man with her whole heart and mind and body. He had taken everything she had to give and walked away from her. "The last time you said you wanted me you were on the rebound." She swallowed thickly. "I was in love with you, but you were in love with another woman. You used me for sex and for revenge."

"What I had with you was different from anything I've had with any other woman, Shavonne. You offered me all your warmth and trust and love, and I was too self-involved to recognize what I was giving up when I let you go."

He hadn't denied her accusations, she noted bleakly. He'd merely side-stepped the issue. It hurt terribly to think of Slade making love to her when he'd been in love with someone else.

"I want you back, Shavonne," he said hoarsely. "I didn't know how much I've missed you until I saw you again. And when I kissed you this morning, all I could think was how good it felt to have you back in my arms. How right it was." His voice deepened possessively. "You're mine, Shavonne."

"There was a time when I would've given anything—

everything—to hear those words from you," she said, her blood pounding in her ears. "But now . . . I—I just don't know. . . ."

"Darling, I understand that you're wary. I hurt you very badly. But that was in the past. I won't hurt you now. I'll take care of your love. This time everything will be all right."

She felt the tension in him, heard the urgency in his voice. She was no longer the innocent she'd been two years ago. She knew that when a man fairly radiated sexual tension and urgency, it was a safe bet his words were more indicative of his need for sex than a promise of love.

"Slade, if you're trying to talk me into going back to your motel room with you, you're wasting your breath. I realize that I lapped up everything you said the first time around, but that was due to naïveté, not stupidity. You taught me a lesson I'm not about to forget."

"Very succinctly put." He tightened his hold on her as he gazed down into her eyes. "I guess I'd forgotten just how frank you can be, Shavonne."

"You once told me that frankness and spontaneity were part of my charm," she reminded him wryly. "I believed you, of course. I believed everything you told me back then."

"Shavonne, sweetheart." He gathered her closer. "I'm not going to hurt you again. This time things will be different, I swear."

Words. Promises. He'd given her those before. Yes, she should definitely push him away and demand to be taken home, she thought. But she could feel the heat and the need in him, and it evoked a primal response deep within her.

"There isn't going to be a 'this time,'" she felt obliged to insist, and realized as she spoke that her voice betrayed her feelings far too well. She sounded as if she were merely offering token resistance not meant to be taken seriously.

Slade picked up on it at once. "There isn't?" he murmured softly, smiling into her eyes. He gently took her earlobe between his teeth and bit lightly, sensuously. She gasped as delicious tingles streaked through her.

"Yes, you like that, don't you sweet?" His tongue began to tease the delicate shell of her ear, and she drew a deep, shuddering breath. "Does it make you feel soft and weak inside, my love? Does it make you want what I want?"

"Slade!" Her cry was full of need and of her dangerous wish to succumb to the moment. Her lashes flickered and she instinctively nestled closer to him.

One of his hands glided down the length of her body and came to rest on her hip, lifting her a little and turning her into him. She felt his hard thigh press against her, felt his strong fingers tighten around the curve of her buttock. A powerful rush of heat surged through her, swelling in her breasts and tightening between her legs.

Her breaths were shallow and rapid and she was trembling all over. She felt hot, feverish, and so alive, her body pulsing with delicious sensations. She loved the feel of his hands upon her. Her body arched into his, seeking more.

It had always been this way, from the first time Slade had touched her two long years ago. She had loved him, and their physical relationship had reflected the depth and the intensity of her feelings for him. With him, her body had experienced the wildest, fiercest pleasure she had ever known.

Was it so very wrong to want to sample that magic again? she wondered dreamily. Her mind seemed to have handed the decision over to her body, which had been too well conditioned to the rapture Slade had given her to pull back now.

"You're so sensual, so responsive." His voice was

ragged as his hand moved slowly to her abdomen. His fingers began a kneading, sensuous massage that fired the ache building there.

"So are you," she whispered, stroking the tanned column of his neck. She loved touching him as much as she loved being touched by him. She savored his maleness: his stubble-roughened jaw, his heady, musky scent, the unyielding hardness of his muscular frame. So different from her, so exotic and exciting and sensually fascinating.

Her head began to spin as his mouth played with hers, opening and closing over it, brushing her lips lightly, sensuously, taking erotic little nips before he slid his tongue into the soft moistness within.

His hands swept slowly over her back, stroking and caressing and pressing her more firmly against the hard wall of his chest. She could feel her breasts swell tightly, and an aching desire for him to touch her there filled her.

As if physically attuned to her, he tentatively brushed her right breast with one hand, and she sighed and trembled, telling him everything he needed to know. Her heart pounded with anticipation as his fingers moved to the buttons of her blouse.

"Shavonne," he said hoarsely. "It's been so long." His fingers shook as he slowly began to undo the buttons, and he fumbled with one or two.

She found this display of vulnerability oddly touching. And quite un-Sladelike. In the past, he had always been the master of his passion, his technique expert and controlled. She had never seen him rendered vulnerable by passion and need. Until this moment . . .

"Do you remember the first time I asked you not to wear a bra?" he whispered as he undid the front clasp of her pale pink brassiere. "How scandalized you were! And how intrigued," he added softly, cupping her bare breasts in both palms.

Sensual memories flooded her while new ones were being created. She heard a soft, sexy moan and realized it had come from her. She clutched his shoulders, sinking her nails into the fabric of his shirt as her control wavered.

"Your skin is like silk. So smooth, so delicate." His thumbs grazed her nipples, which were already hard and tight and aching. "Shavonne, it's going to be so good between us. This time—this time . . ." His voice trailed off as he caught one nipple between his thumb and forefinger and gently caressed it, watching her arch at the exquisite pleasure he was giving her.

He bent to kiss the throbbing peak, taking the taut pink bud into his mouth. The warm, moist suction of his lips sent her spiraling into a maelstrom of desire.

"Slade," she sighed, threading her fingers through his hair as she held his mouth to her. "Slade, it feels so good."

"Oh, yes, sweetheart." Slade groaned, wildly, incredibly aroused by her words. She'd never been inhibited in expressing her pleasure. He hadn't been feeding her a line when he'd said that her frankness and spontaneity were all part of the charm she held for him.

"Do you know how it makes me feel to hear you say that, darling?" he asked. "To know that I can arouse you and give you pleasure?" He circled one nipple with his tongue and she cried out his name. "You make me feel powerful and sexy and very much a man. You've always done that for me, Shavonne. You're so feminine and warm."

She'd been exactly what he had needed after Lexie's crushing blow to his masculine ego. He had come to Shavonne and she had restored his confidence in himself. She'd made him feel like an extraordinary, irresistible lover, the most desirable, wonderful man in the world.

And how had he repaid her?

Even in the throes of passion, Slade felt guilt and regret slice into him. He was going to make it up to her, he promised himself. He would prove to her beyond any doubt just how very special she was to him.

His hand slipped under her skirt and smoothed over the warm skin of her thighs. He was delighted that the day had been hot enough and her legs were tanned enough for her to dispense with panty hose. His fingers skimmed over the sheer silky material of her panties and his pulses hammered. He wanted to lose himself in her, to feel her sweet softness envelop him as he filled her. He wanted her, all of her, with an intensity unlike anything he had ever known.

And he could have her. She was clinging to him, her surrender implicit. He could take her here in the car and ease this taut, aching urgency now, *now*. . .

His mouth closed hungrily over hers. His kiss was hot and slow and deep, unleashing the current of fire flaming through him.

Shavonne felt almost faint from the intensity of his kiss, from the wild demands her own body was making. She clung to him, twisting restlessly with need and abandon. His hand was sliding sensuously over her thighs, her bottom, her abdomen, coming tantalizingly near, but never quite touching the throbbing center of her femininity.

His tongue was in her mouth, boldly stroking and seeking, and she writhed as passion surged and built, heightening the torrents of sensation rushing through her. She moved her legs slightly apart in silent invitation, and the liquid heat of her passion poured through her as his hand finally found her.

"Slade," she moaned in a plea of want and need.

Euphoria bubbled through his veins. He could have her; she was his for the taking. He gazed down at her. She was small and soft in his arms, her face flushed, her slender fingers clutching his shoulders. She looked so utterly desirable—and so utterly vulnerable.

He knew in that moment he had to stop. It was moving too fast, and he didn't want her to think he was using her for his own quick physical satisfaction. He never wanted to give her cause to believe that again. He would prove to her by his actions that he wanted to give to her, not take, that from now on he was putting her needs before his own.

The ache between Shavonne's legs was pulsing uncontrollably, and she moved wantonly against his hand. She whimpered as his fingers slipped under the lacy pink edges of her panties, then shivered deliciously as he touched her intimately, stroking and rubbing and probing delicately, teasing her, arousing her until she thought she was going to scream.

Then he slipped his fingers inside her as his tongue stroked deeply in her mouth. The simultaneous sensations were shattering, and the passionate firestorm burning within her flared to flash point. Sparks showered through her body as she exploded into rapture.

Slade held her tightly, murmuring her name and watching her with possessive gray eyes as the spasms of ecstasy rippled through her. Wrapped in his arms, she drifted slowly, languorously, back to earth. The fire in her body had receded to a warm glow, and she snuggled closer, drowsy and relaxed, savoring the security of Slade's embrace.

His lips brushed her temple. "I want you so much, Shavonne. More than I've ever wanted anyone in my entire life."

She gazed up at him. His eyes were intense, his mouth drawn into a taut line. Her mind began to clear and she roused slowly from the sweet torpor of sexual satisfaction. She felt the heat and hardness of his straining desire. The tension in his body was in direct contrast to the blissful languor flowing through hers. She frowned, and the first vestiges of shame and doubt pricked her. "I . . . um . . ." She ran her tongue nervously over her lips and a slow blush spread from her cheeks to the tips of her toes. *What now*? she wondered, a little wildly. She really hadn't intended to let things get this far, but . . . She closed her eyes. But she had. And now, now . . .

"Don't worry, I'm not going to drag you off to the motel," he said dryly, and her blush deepened for he had voiced her thoughts aloud. He straightened her clothes, his hands both tender and efficient. The glitter in his eyes told her how much restraint he was exerting. "Unless you insist, of course," he added, and when her eyes widened, he kissed her cheeks, her nose, and her chin, then said softly, "I was just teasing, sweetheart. The only place I'm taking you is to the mall to buy suitcases and to pick up Tara."

Shavonne was thoroughly bemused. "But you didn't—" She inhaled sharply and started over. "You haven't—" She broke off, averting her face.

"Don't be shy, honey." He tipped her chin upward, forcing her to meet his gaze. "I don't want you to ever feel shy or embarrassed with me. What happened between us tonight was natural and right— for both of us."

Was it? she wondered, mesmerized by the warm blue lights in his eyes. She was feeling guilty that he had pleasured her so thoroughly while his own obvious need was still unsatisfied. The Slade of two years ago wouldn't have called a halt at such a crucial time; she was more than certain of that. He had given her fulfillment then, but he had also always taken his own.

A small sigh escaped from her lips. However she read the situation, she was sure to be wrong. She was uncommonly adept at misreading Slade's signals and intentions. She wished she understood men, but the opposite sex remained as mysterious to her as an alien species. If only her father had stuck around, if only she'd had a brother or her only brother-in-law hadn't been such a subhuman terror, maybe she'd have an inkling to the workings of the male mind.

Slade's voice intruded upon her thoughts. "I think it's time for us to be on our way. We have a lot to do this evening." He disengaged himself from their embrace and straightened in his seat.

When she started to slide across the seat to the passenger side, he caught her arm, stilling her. "Sit here, beside me," he invited, taking her hand and laying it on his thigh.

He started the car and pulled back onto the road, then switched on the radio. A soft, romantic ballad filled the car, and Shavonne knew she would always associate that song with this night. Unconsciously, her fingers flexed on his thigh and she felt the hard muscles beneath the smooth fabric.

He dropped his hand to cover hers. "I'm glad you're coming to Texas with me, sweetheart," he said huskily.

"Texas." She swallowed. "I'd almost forgotten about that." In truth, she'd forgotten about everything but herself and Slade in their own private world. She felt the warm strength of his hand over hers, and turned her head to stare at him thoughtfully. "Slade, if I ask you a question, will you answer me honestly?"

"Yes, of course I will, darling."

"A few minutes ago, when you said that you wanted me more than you've ever wanted anyone . . . did you mean you wanted me personally? Or did you mean you wanted sex?"

"Shavonne, sweetheart, I meant I wanted *you*." Slade entwined his fingers firmly with hers. Did she distrust him that much, he wondered, or was her feminine confidence that shaky? Either possibility was equally disturbing to him. Had he done that to her?

"I just want to get things straight this time," she said. "Am I standing in for someone else? And if that's the case—"

"You're not standing in for anyone. No one else will do. I want you. Only you, Shavonne." He realized how true it was as he spoke the words. Lifting her hand to his mouth, he brushed his lips over her palm.

She shivered at the sensuous caress. "What about your fiancée?"

"I don't have a fiancée."

"Your ex-fiancée."

He thought of Lexie and their cat-and-mouse relationship. It suddenly seemed trivial and immature. He'd never seriously entertained the notion of taking her back, although he'd enjoyed allowing her to think that he might. His masculine ego and shattered pride had gloried in turning the tables on her. He frowned. These past two years hadn't been illuminating ones for his character, he silently admitted. He'd begun pretending to be a rat and had ended up becoming one.

"She's out of my life, Shavonne," he said firmly. It was time to put an end to the juvenile game-playing. He no longer cared about punishing Lexie; he no longer cared about Lexie at all. It was Shavonne he cared about, Shavonne he wanted. Had it been her all along and he'd been too blinded by ego and pride to realize it?

There was a moment's silence. Then Shavonne asked, "When she broke your engagement, was it to marry someone else?"

He shook his head. "No. She broke the engagement for a fling with a pretty boy actor in a regional theater company."

"I see." Shavonne nodded gravely. "That's worse than leaving you to marry someone else."

His smile was wry. "Is it?"

"Oh, yes. Infinitely worse," she assured him. "I can understand why you were so mad. And I—I've decided that I forgive you for taking it out on me."

"You're very generous, Shavonne," he said quietly. "You're sweet and strong and loyal and loving, and I—"

"But I'm not ready to pick up where we left off," she cut in swiftly.

He glanced at her. "Message received," he murmured. She had obviously gone back to being confused and wary, perhaps even more so than before, and he congratulated himself on his restraint. Though she'd responded to him with uninhibited passion, had he rushed her into intercourse, she would have been sick with regret. "I understand, Shavonne, but I'm not giving up." On the contrary, he was just beginning. "I want you to understand that."

"As long as you understand that I'm not a stupid little tramp from the wrong side of the tracks who you can tumble into bed whenever you get the urge for sex."

"Shavonne, I've never thought of you that way. Never." The anguish in her trembling voice pierced him. "I know you won't believe me if I tell you that I love you, but—"

"You're right," she said flatly. "I won't believe you. You said it before too easily."

"Time wounds all heels," he murmured. "Great-Aunt Augusta called that one right."

"She said that to you?"

"Before I left for Houston that summer two years ago. It was her parting shot. One I richly deserved."

He stared pensively ahead and she squeezed his hand. "I don't think you're a heel, Slade. I'm beginning to believe that you really are a nice guy who was hurt and frustrated and tired of finishing last. I just wish you hadn't picked me to use for target practice when you decided to avenge yourself."

He slipped his arm around her shoulder, continuing to steer the car with his left hand. "Does that mean you're willing to forget about the past and start over, Shavonne?" he asked huskily.

"I don't know about starting over. I'm too mixed up to think about that now."

"I'll take the fact that you're mixed up as a positive sign." He smiled at her. "Ambivalence certainly beats abject hatred and disgust."

"Just about *anything* beats abject hatred and disgust. Simply because I don't hate you doesn't mean that I—"

"Shavonne, at this point, I'm willing to take one small step at a time with you."

She eyed him curiously for several moments, then a small smile lit her face.

"Private joke?" he asked. "Or will you share it with me?"

She shrugged. "I was just thinking that I like the new, improved version of Slade Ramsey better than the counterpart I knew before."

Slade felt lighter than air. Who would have believed that such a diffident admission from her would make him want to shout with pure happiness? He cast a quick glance at her. She was gazing out the windshield, a thoughtful expression on her face. He grinned. She was his, all right, she just didn't realize it yet. It would be his continuing pleasure to convince her of that fact.

Seven

Even allowing for the extra hours gained by the change in time zones, it was late when Slade and the Bradys arrived at the Houston airport that night. He rounded up their luggage and hustled them into another rental, this one a van big enough to accommodate them all.

Exhausted from the excitement of the trip, Shavonne's sisters and nieces slept while Slade steered the van through the Houston traffic, which Shavonne found amazingly heavy for the time of night.

"You don't see this much traffic on our interstate back home unless it's the Saturday of the WVU-Pitt football game," she said, staring at the unbroken stream of cars. She was physically tired, but too mentally wired to consider sleeping. And she was aware that Slade's presence was generating the electricity that was humming through her.

She was sitting in the front next to him, her seat separated from his by the gear console. She'd sat next to him in the plane during the long flight to Houston, and they'd talked and laughed like old friends the entire time. It was an interesting paradox. She'd felt relaxed and comfortable with him, yet being so close to him evoked the same exciting and potent effect he'd always had upon her senses. When she was with Slade, he filled her world.

It was a disturbing admission for her to make, for it meant the reverse corollary was also true—that her life was empty when he wasn't in it. She'd already had to make that painful adjustment once. To have to do it again . . .

"Are you nervous about being here, Shavonne?" he asked, interrupting her anxious reverie.

"A little," she lied.

"Only a little?"

"A lot," she admitted with a sheepish smile. "Leaving home to fly across the country isn't exactly an everyday occurrence for us."

"It's a decision you won't regret. I'm going to do everything in my power to convince you of that."

He smiled, an incredibly sexy smile of masculine challenge.

A smile that made Shavonne's heart turn over. In his power . . .

"Where are we going tonight?" she asked breathlessly, as the full realization of her dependency upon him struck her with full force. She had no money; she and her family were thousands of miles away from their home and everyone they knew. Slade had complete control of her here. She was indeed in his power. And she had given him that power by agreeing to let him bring them here. *Had she lost her mind?* Panic set in as she realized just how little thought she'd given to the consequences of impulsive actions.

"I've arranged for you to stay at the Park Mall Hotel tonight," he said in a calm, soothing tone she knew was meant to reassure her. "It's adjacent to the Ramsey Park Mall."

She was not reassured. She recognized the name of the mall. It was the one that Slade insisted was partly built on the property she owned. What if it was true? She allowed herself to entertain the possibility for the first time, then quickly dismissed it as her panic heightened. It couldn't be true! What would she do if it was? She knew nothing of great wealth. She'd only wanted enough money to pay their bills and update the kitchen!

"Doesn't Houston have a Ramada Inn?" she asked nervously. At least she was familiar with that, even if it did conjure up memories of Slade's room in Morgantown, the place she'd given herself to him, time after time. Her body felt warm, and she knew it wasn't because of the Texas heat. "I think I'd rather stay there."

"You don't have to worry about a thing, Shavonne. I'm going to take care of you," Slade said firmly, and proceeded to drive to the spectacular mall and hotel complex lit with the Ramsey name.

His actions seemed to reinforce his power over her a thousandfold. She gulped and said nothing as a uniformed doorman and three bellhops leaped forward to do Slade's bidding. She was suddenly in a world that previously hadn't existed for her, with Slade Ramsey as her only ally.

The Bradys were awed as they were deferentially ushered to the enormous two-bedroom suite Slade had commandeered for them. All five sisters were wide-eyed and silent; they had been since first glimpsing the luxuriously appointed hotel lobby and sumptuous adjoining mall.

Megan was the first to find her voice. "There's a crib for Courtney in one of the bedrooms. Do you want me to put her in it, Erin?"

"I'll do it," Erin said quickly. "I want to get Carrie Beth into bed, too. She's asleep on her feet."

"I'll help you," Tara added.

"Me too," Colleen and Megan chorused.

Everyone was desperate to find some bearings, Shavonne thought. Putting the little ones to bed was a familiar procedure offering security in this strange new world. She knew exactly how her sisters felt. She wished she could join them. But Slade had hold of her hand, and he didn't release it when her sisters and nieces disappeared into the bedroom.

Slade was studying Shavonne thoughtfully. She looked shell-shocked, he mused. Perhaps she was, poor baby. He had rushed her out of her safe, familiar little world into . . . the world of the Ramseys. And even a born-and-bred Ramsey like himself could feel adrift in it.

Well, she would have him as her anchor, he vowed silently. After tonight, he would move the family into his own house in West University, a shady residential area near Rice University. The girls were undoubtedly intimidated by the size and splendor of the opulent hotel, and they would find life here difficult and restrictive, especially with the two little ones. Tomorrow he would rent baby furniture and do whatever else it took to make his house feel like home for the Bradys. And especially for Shavonne.

"I'll come for you tomorrow morning, Shavonne," he said quietly. "Will ten o'clock be too early? I know you and the girls are exhausted."

Shavonne's stomach lurched convulsively. "You're leaving? And you aren't going to—to—"

"I told you I'm not going to hustle you into bed. Is that what you thought? That I'd make you sleep with me tonight?"

She faced him, exhaustion and anxiety making her reckless. "You could have. There's nothing to stop you from doing whatever you want, and you know it."

"Do you want to make love with me tonight, Shavonne?"

Her face burned at the blunt question. Suppose she were to say yes? It was disturbing to admit how tempted she was to do just that. But she didn't dare. It was too soon and too much was happening, and her judgment around Slade Ramsey had always been questionable at best. "No!" she said sternly to herself as well as him.

"Well, then, that's what's stopping me."

"It never stopped you before," she felt compelled to remind him. "There were times during our . . . affair when I didn't want to be whisked immediately into bed, when I wanted to talk with you, to spend nonsexual time with you."

"And I would sweep your protests aside and make love to you because we always did what I wanted, when I wanted." His eyes met hers. "I told you that things were going to be different this time, Shavonne. This time I'm not going to keep an emotional distance between us by silencing you with sex."

Silencing her with sex, she repeated to herself. Yes, he had done that, hadn't he? But their limited relationship hadn't been all his fault. She was beginning to realize that now. She wasn't blameless because she had allowed him to use her. She'd always given in to the passion of the moment, acquiescing eagerly. Hadn't she done just that earlier tonight in the car?

She drew a deep breath and faced him squarely. "Sex was a big part of our relationship, Slade. Maybe that's all we had between us. And if that's the case, it would be foolish even to think about starting over."

It was hard for Slade to remain calm and collected when every instinct he possessed was urging him to pull her into his arms and kiss her senseless. He was tired of her uncertainty. He wanted to make her want what he wanted. Once he got her into bed . . .

That was the way he'd handled her during their affair, he reminded himself. Silencing her with sex. He wanted more than the one-dimensional relationship his coolly arrogant alter ego had had with her.

"If you're uncertain about us," he said, "then maybe we should declare a moratorium on sex." It was the kind of thing a caring and honest nice guy would say, he knew. And that's what he was, what he had to convince Shavonne that he was. A man worthy of her trust. "We know we're good together in bed. Let's see what else we have going for us."

Maybe she would refuse, he thought hopefully. Maybe she would tell him that they could do both— make love *and* develop a new relationship.

"A moratorium on sex," she repeated. "Yes, I think that's a good idea." She half-hoped he would change his mind and disagree with her. That he would snatch her into his arms and . . . *silence her with sex? Sweep away her common sense with passion?*

No, they'd played those games too many times before, she told herself. It was time she took some responsibility for herself, instead of seeking refuge in the seductive fantasy of being swept away. She'd told Slade she was all grown up; it was time she proved it.

They stared at each other for a long moment. Slade was the first to break the tension-charged silence. "That's it, then. As of right now, we'll officially declare a—"

"Moratorium on sex," Shavonne chimed in, so that they said it together.

They both laughed self-consciously.

Slade cupped her shoulders and drew her toward him. "I put my card with my telephone number on it on the nightstand. If you need anything at all tonight, I want you to call me." He bent to touch his lips to her forehead. "And if I don't hear from you tonight, I'll see you at ten tomorrow."

She raised her face to his. He was looking at her in such a way. . . . Her pulses raced. His gaze was warm and tender, his lips curved into a smile that sent little ripples of heat coursing through her.

"Good night, sweetheart." He slid his hands from her shoulders and along the length of her arms in a long, slow caress. Then he turned and quickly left the suite.

Bemused, bewildered, Shavonne stood alone, staring at the door he had closed behind him. A moratorium on sex? How could it work when she melted every time he touched her, every time he looked at her?

She was grateful when Colleen bounded into the room, distracting her from her disturbing thoughts.

"This place is incredible!" Colleen cried gleefully. "Wait'll you see the bathroom. There's one of those big round tubs in it—a Jacuzzi, I think. I wonder if we dare to use it?"

"Of course you can use it, Colleen." Tara drifted in to join them. "This is our room, for tonight anyway."

Colleen sighed blissfully. "It's wonderful, pretending to be rich! I'm so glad Slade brought us here. He's such a nice guy, isn't he, Shavonne?"

A nice guy, Shavonne thought. That was exactly what Slade claimed to be. She had to smile. It hadn't described the man she'd known two years ago, but it fit the man she'd been with today. The generous, understanding man who'd agreed not to rush her sexually. "Yes, Colleen, he's a nice guy," she said softly.

"I wonder why he's being so nice to us," Tara said musingly. "Because of the land?"

"Maybe," said Erin. She'd entered the room with Megan. "But I think both Mama and Aunt Augusta have already given us the reason why."

"They have?" Shavonne tilted her head quizzically. "What is it?"

"You're playing hard to get this time, Shavonne," Erin replied. "I think Slade thought he could get you back simply by crooking his little finger, but you surprised him. You showed him that it wasn't going to be so easy, that he couldn't have what he wanted. And as Mama used to say—"

"A man always wants what he can't have," the younger girls chorused.

Shavonne thought back to her impassioned and abandoned response to Slade earlier that evening, in the car parked along the deserted Star City road. She felt hot, as if burning with fever. One thing was certain, she hadn't been playing hard to get then. Slade had to know that she would have surrendered to him.

Was it possible he didn't know how easily he could have had her? Did he think she was unattainable, and had that spiked his interest? And now they had a moratorium on sex. She sighed. Was she playing hard to get without even knowing it?

"Well, Megan said, grinning, "if playing hard to get is what got us this trip to Houston and a night in this fabulous hotel, then I'm all for it." Keep up the good work, Shavonne."

Slade arrived the next morning a few minutes before ten. He was accompanied by a distinguished looking silver-haired woman who was wearing the female version of the pin-stripe suit Slade had on. Both carried sleek attaché cases.

Shavonne stared at them. She'd never seen Slade in a suit. He looked rich and powerful and sophisticated—and about as accessible as a head of state. She smoothed the pleats of her yellow and black polka dot dress—her best—and wished she didn't feel like a nervous schoolgirl.

"Shavonne!" Slade greeted her warmly. He took both her hands in his and lightly brushed her cheek with his lips in a friendly, almost brotherly, kiss. "I see you've had breakfast." He glanced at the table stacked with empty dishes in the center of the room.

"At seven-thirty," she said. "Courtney and Carrie Beth woke up starving."

"We watch *Hotel* on TV, so we know all about room service," Megan said blithely as she came into the room. She was wearing one of the new outfits Slade had bought for her. The skirt, blouse, and cotton vest had been expensive and looked it, Shavonne thought. She compared it to her discount store dress, which hadn't been expensive. It didn't look as if it had been either.

"Shavonne, Megan," Slade said, "I'd like you to meet Sissy Timmons. She's an attorney who's interested in taking you on as clients."

"So pleased to meet you both," Sissy Timmons said with a friendliness that immediately put Shavonne at ease. She shook hands with Shavonne, then Megan.

"I've shown Sissy Great-Aunt Augusta's will and the deed to the land," Slade continued. "She's studied them carefully and found both documents to be legally binding and valid."

Shavonne looked bewildered. "Of course they're valid. Why would I give you fake papers?"

"It's just that this is an unusual situation, Shavonne," Sissy explained smoothly. "It isn't often that an unknown party inherits such a lucrative parcel of land, the rest of which is held exclusively by family members. And when that family happens to be the Ramseys. . . . Well, I wanted to make sure the documents you held were legally impeccable. And I'm pleased to say that they are."

"And now can I sell my land to Slade?" Shavonne asked hopefully.

"I suggest that we thoroughly explore all the possibilities before we even think about selling to anyone, Shavonne," Sissy said firmly. "First on the agenda is to talk with Quentin Ramsey."

"Dad would like you to meet with him at home this morning, Shavonne," Slade added.

In point of fact, he thought, Quentin Ramsey had demanded the meeting. Slade thought back to his father's response to his phone call earlier this morning . . .

"Shavonne Brady is here in Houston?" Quentin was clearly not pleased with the news. "But I sent two of our attorneys to that godforsaken town of hers this morning with papers for her to sign."

Quentin was even less pleased with Slade's reply. "Shavonne won't be signing anything without her lawyer's advice, Dad. Sissy Timmons is representing her." Slade braced himself for his father's reaction.

It was as explosive as he'd predicted. "*Sissy Timmons?* That insurgent, liberal, feminist maverick pirhana!" Slade thought there might've been a few dozen more adjectives, but he stopped listening. He knew his father's opinion of Sissy Timmons, but had asked her to represent the Bradys in spite of it. Sissy Timmons *was* a cunning maverick who'd proven that she couldn't be bought or bullied by anyone. Including the Ramsey Family.

"Look, Courtney, here's that daddy!"

The excited little voice drew Slade back to the present. Carrie Beth came running into the room, resplendent in a white dress with yellow duck smocking, her blond curls pulled into two beribboned ponytails. Courtney toddled after her, dressed identically, except for the bow that was taped to her short, wispy, baby-fine hair.

"Da!" Courtney echoed. Carrie Beth effusively threw her arms around Slade's legs. Courtney immediately followed suit.

"The children are adorable," Sissy said warmly.

"Yes, they are, aren't they?" He scooped both little girls up in his arms. "Maybe we should bring them along to this meeting," he added, looking thoughtfully at the five Brady sisters standing together in the room. His gaze came to rest on Shavonne, and a surge of delight filled him. She was so wholesome and lovely and sweet. All the girls were. Who could resist them?

"I think everyone should go to this meeting" he said decisively. "Shavonne and her sisters and these two little munchkins as well." The Ramseys were tough, but he felt sure that the Bradys would win his family's hearts. After all, he was a Ramsey and they'd certainly won his.

"I like Sissy Timmons," Shavonne told Slade as he drove the rented van along Interstate 610 toward River Oaks, home of Quentin and Nola Ramsey. The rest of the Bradys were settled in the back seats of the van, and Sissy Timmons was following in her fawn-colored Mercedes. "She reminds me of a younger, pin-stripe edition of Aunt Augusta."

Slade smiled. "Sissy's been quite successful. She's sharp and she's shrewd and she likes to champion the underdog." Which the Bradys definitely were when pitted against the Ramseys, he added silently.

"Slade, the land . . . It really *is* worth twenty-five million dollars, isn't it?"

"Yes. Are you finally ready and willing to accept that fact?"

"And Aunt Augusta . . . knew what it was worth? She knew all about the mall when she willed it to me?"

"Absolutely. I guess she decided to have the last laugh in her feud with brother Harlan by snubbing his family and blithely leaving the property to her young neighbors."

"Knowing full well it would drive her poor nephew up the wall!" Shavonne sighed. "I feel like I'm living in a waking dream. Things like this don't happen to normal, ordinary people like me. But here we are in Houston and I've seen the mall and Sissy Timmons is perfectly serious about being my lawyer."

"You're a very wealthy young woman, Shavonne," Slade said. "The income the property generates comes from the rent the merchants pay to the mall owners. You'll be getting a quarter of that—approximately a quarter of a million dollars a month."

Her jaw dropped and he grinned at her astonishment. "Think you can manage to live on that?"

She tried to smile, but it turned into an apprehensive frown instead. "I know I should be happy, but I'm scared, Slade. I don't know if I can handle the responsibility of all that money. Our lives will change so much . . . We're used to scrimping and budgeting down to the last penny. What if suddenly getting so rich makes us go haywire?"

"It'll take more than getting rich to make you go haywire." He cast her a warmly affectionate smile. "I'm absolutely certain that you'll adjust to this situation as you have to everything else fate has thrown your way—with strength and dignity." His voice deepened. "With humor and love."

His smile went straight to her heart and his words made her glow. "Thank you," she said softly.

He laid his hand on hers and her fingers curled around his. He was about to lift her hand to his mouth to kiss each finger, then place her hand on his thigh, firmly under his. She was about to press his palm to her lips and rub it against her cheek.

Then they both remembered their moratorium on sex and simultaneously decided that such actions were definitely sexy.

Slade withdrew his hand at the same moment that Shavonne drew back hers. They exchanged quick, weak smiles.

•   •   •

River Oaks, the bastion of Houston's ultra-rich, stunned the Bradys with its opulence and grandeur. The Ramseys' home wasn't merely a house, it was a mansion fronted with a lawn the size of a baseball field. It had an Olympic-sized swimming pool and a forty-foot stone fireplace. There were thick carpets and heavy drapes and impressive furniture upholstered with brocade. There were polished tables loaded with precious art objects—miniature portraits, enamel snuff boxes, exquisite figurines, and vases filled with fresh flowers. The walls were hung with tapestries and original oils. Uniformed servants seemed to be everywhere.

Shavonne held Carrie Beth and Erin hung on to Courtney. They didn't dare set the children down; two active little ones could demolish the fragile untouchables and antique furniture. Tara, Colleen, and Megan stared dazedly around the gigantic living room, which had more square feet than their entire house in Star City.

Shavonne stood between Slade and Sissy Timmons and kept stealing glances at them both. Sissy appeared cool and calm, as if she dealt with a purple-faced, table-pounding Quentin Ramsey every day. As if the dagger-glares from Nola Ramsey amused her. As if Slade's brothers, Rad and Jed, didn't look capable of murder as they pinned the Bradys with deadly, gray-eyed stares while issuing their threats and ultimatums.

Shavonne's gaze was also repeatedly drawn to Vanessa Ramsey, Slade's sister. She looked like a high-fashion model, tall and sleek and slender, in a striking indigo jumpsuit with matching indigo high-heeled shoes. Slade had told her that his sister was just her age, twenty-three. It was hard to believe. Vanessa was so regal and polished and sophisticated, Shavonne felt like an awkward twelve-year-old in comparison.

Quentin, Rad, and Jed were firing off statements and threats with machine-gun speed, one jumping in before another finished speaking. Shavonne cast an apprehensive glance at Slade. His mouth was drawn in a tight line. On the drive over here, he'd warned her to expect some fireworks. He'd grown up amidst his family's theatrics, he'd told her. They could be tiresome, but he always believed the old saw that their bark was worse than their bite.

Shavonne wasn't so sure. Her younger sisters were clearly terrified by the hostility radiating from every Ramsey but Slade. The girls looked ready to run at any given moment. Shavonne shifted Carrie Beth in her arms. The little girl clung tightly, her face buried in Shavonne's shoulder.

Slade listened to his family rant and rave with a growing sense of gloom. He'd never felt so alienated from them. Their behavior was atrocious, a kind of collective Ramsey temper tantrum. He was thoroughly disillusioned. His family had seen the Bradys and hadn't relented. They hadn't been moved by the hardship these five beautiful sisters had known. They'd scarcely glanced at the adorable baby girls. It was depressing for him to have to acknowledge that his family would still cheat Shavonne and her family if they could pull it off.

But he and Sissy Timmons weren't about to let that happen. Feeling inordinately protective, he moved closer to Shavonne and put his arm around her waist, drawing her against him. It wasn't a sexual move, he assured himself, it was a comforting one.

Shavonne seemed to understand. She leaned into his strength, apparently appreciative of his show of support. Carrie Beth, secure in her aunt's arms, was immediately diverted by his tie and her proximity to it. She reached over to touch the unfamiliar item of masculine apparel.

Shavonne's eyes met his, and they smiled at each other, sharing a quiet, private moment in the midst of the tension and chaos.

Unfortunately, Vanessa also observed those special smiles and viewed the small exchange as further evidence of her brother's collusion with the enemy. "Slade, how can you betray the family this way?" she demanded shrilly. "How can you align yourself with this—this thieving band of refugees?"

"Shavonne has legally inherited Augusta Ramsey's property and is entitled to its full value," Slade said flatly. He'd been making that same bald pronouncement every time there was an opening for him to speak. And it wasn't winning him any popularity contests among the Ramseys.

"You're too soft, Slade!" Vanessa said, her voice rising. "We never should've sent *you* to deal with this marauding bunch of bleached blond pirates!"

"We don't bleach our hair," Megan dared to say.

Vanessa rolled her eyes heavenward, then started back in on her brother. "You really disappoint me, Slade. I thought you'd finally become a real man, like Daddy and Rad and Jed, but you haven't changed a bit! You're still the same old Eagle Scout, aren't you? Still Mr. Nice Guy. But now you expect the rest of the Ramseys to finish last along with you!"

Shavonne gaped at Vanessa scarcely believing what she had heard. How could anyone so gorgeous be so viperish? Her heart went out to Slade. How must he feel, being attacked so cruelly by his only sister?

"Slade is everything a real man should be!" she said, her dark eyes flashing with anger. "He's strong and brave and he wants to do the right thing. He—"

"Strong and brave?" Jed interrupted with a sardonic laugh. "Those are hardly the words I'd use to describe a man who's soft-headed enough to hand over twenty-five million dollars to a trashy little blonde. What kind of hold do you have over my addlebrained brother, baby?"

"Shut up, Jed," Slade said. "Attack me, if you want, but leave Shavonne alone."

"How gallant!" Jed drawled. "This girl obviously has you spellbound, Slade. Why, I wonder? Is she that amazing in bed?"

Slade reddened as fury surged through him. "I'm not going to stand by and listen to you insult Shavonne this way."

Before Shavonne could exhale, Slade was across the room. He managed to catch his younger brother by surprise. Slade had always been the family's equanimous peacemaker; no one expected him to erupt in a rage. Everyone watched in shock as he grabbed Jed by the shoulders, hauled him out of his chair, and shoved him against the wall. The resounding thump seemed to echo throughout the huge room.

Tara, Colleen, and Megan began to cry. Carrie Beth started to scream. Erin turned white and clutched Shavonne's arm. "I feel sick," she croaked hoarsely. "Here, take Courtney." She thrust the baby into Shavonne's arms and rushed from the room.

"Erin, wait for me!" Shavonne called. Since Erin's disastrous marriage to the bellicose Charlie Ray Tyler, physical violence literally made her ill. Shavonne, her arms full with both nieces, ran after Erin, the three youngest girls at her heals.

Shouts and shrieks and the crashing sound of breaking china followed them into the spacious marble and tiled hallway. The Bradys didn't stop running until they were outside with Erin, whom they found pale and trembling as she leaned against the side of the house.

"Let's get out here!" exclaimed Tara. "This place is an insane asylum!"

"I agree," Slade said as he joined them, his expression grim. "And we're leaving it now. Sissy Timmons will deal with my father and his lawyers from here on in." He took Carrie Beth and Courtney from Shavonne and started toward the van.

"You can tell them that Shavonne won't sell her land to them for a trillion dollars!" a furious Megan yelled after him. "Aunt Augusta was right. Her brother Harlan's family really are dirty-dealing scoundrels!"

"Aunt Augusta hardly even knew her brother Harlan's family," Shavonne reminded Megan. "And Slade is one of Harlan's grandsons. He's not a dirty-dealing scoundrel, and I doubt if he appreciates you calling his family such names."

"I bet he doesn't mind," Megan said. "They're awful! They tried to cheat us out of millions of dollars that Aunt Augusta wanted us to have. And they have the nerve to call *us* pirates!"

"They said we took advantage of Aunt Augusta when she was old and sick and that we tricked her into willing us the land," Colleen said indignantly.

"And we know it isn't true," Shavonne pointed out as they reached the van. Slade had already strapped the two little ones into their car seats.

Her voice shaking with rage, Megan burst out, "That witch Vanessa said you were a scheming little cheat who dressed like you shopped at rummage sales, Shavonne!"

I'm sorry for this entire debacle," Slade said, taking both of Shavonne's hands in his. "I shouldn't have brought you all here and exposed you to their venom, but I honestly didn't think it would go this way. I thought once they saw you, once they saw the kids . . ." He shook his head. "My mother loves children. I thought she'd take one look at Carrie Beth and Courtney and want to grandmother them. I thought if Dad and Jed and Rad saw who they were trying to cheat, they would have a change of heart . . . at least I hoped they would. As for Vanessa, I know she's spoiled, but I've always assumed that basically, she's generous and fair-minded. Today is the first time I've seen her as a totally shallow, selfish shrew."

He looked so grim, so sad and disheartened, Shavonne wanted to comfort him, to ease the pain in his eyes. She knew he loved his family, and who understood family loyalty better than she? Impulsively, she moved closer, squeezing his hands and gazing up at him.

"It's not your fault, Slade. And it takes more than a few nasty remarks to hurt us Bradys." A sudden grin curved her mouth. "Besides, at least one of them is true. Sometimes we do shop at rummage sales."

She turned to her sisters. "We've gotten some great buys at those sales, right? Maybe Vanessa would like to come along with us sometime."

"Sure she would," Tara said with caustic sweetness, "On the same day that the President gives Alaska back to the Russians." They all laughed together.

"Ah, Shavonne, I've never met anyone like you," Slade said huskily as he pulled her into his arms. For a strictly friendly, non-sexual hug.

Shavonne glowed. If she'd had any lingering doubts about Slade's inherent nice-guyness, they were forever banished. He had hoped that his family would respond to her sisters and small nieces as he himself had—with generosity and kindness. Slade was a good person who expected to find goodness in others. What a shame his horrid family had disillusioned him!

"And I want to thank you for defending me," he added, smiling down at her. "I've never had anyone leap to my defense the way you did in there."

Having met that crew, Shavonne could believe it. They'd probably sided with his heartless fiancée when she'd jilted him. The fire-breathing Ramseys would have no use for a nice guy.

"I'm on your side," she said. "They'd better watch what they say about you around me!" She hugged him fiercely. It was strange, but she felt protective of him, the way she did toward her sisters and nieces. She wanted to chase away anyone or anything that might hurt him. She wanted him to be happy. She wanted to make him happy.

Her heart gave an odd little thump. Two years ago, when she'd thought herself so in love with Slade, she hadn't felt this protective tenderness toward him. She'd never felt that he needed her help and support like she'd known he had today.

She was, she realized, seeing Slade as a *person* for the first time ever. Not as a baffling, inexplicable male whose thoughts were beyond her comprehension. Not as a mysterious alien, wildly different from herself. She understood what he was feeling and could relate it to her own feelings. For the first time ever, she saw a man as a fellow human being, and not some elusive creature with whom she must constantly be on her guard.

Her eyes met his and something unseen, something intangible, yet very real passed between them. For that moment, everything that kept them apart receded into a hazy background. Despite family conflicts and class differences, despite their stormy past with its confusing myriad of games and strategies and their current uncertainty, for that moment Shavonne and Slade were very much one in mind and spirit.

Eight

"Shavonne, there's Sissy Timmons," Colleen said and waved to the woman briskly approaching their table at the Ramsey Park Mall food court.

Shavonne rose to her feet and greeted her attorney with a warm hug. "Hello, Sissy. Is this a coincidence or did you know we were here?"

Sissy slipped a maternal arm around Shavonne's waist. "It's not a coincidence, honey. I wouldn't voluntarily eat in this place." She gave an exaggerated shudder. "The Ramseys can dress it up all they want and give it a fancy name, but every one of these fast food stalls serves plastic food guaranteed to bring on acute indigestion."

The Brady sisters laughed. "It's wonderful food, Sissy," insisted Megan. "We eat here almost every day. In the two weeks since we've been in Houston, we've sampled every stand in the court."

Sissy sighed dramatically. "Ah, the endurance—and the steel-lined stomachs—of the young." She turned to Shavonne and smiled. "I stopped off at your suite with some papers for you to sign, and one of the hotel maids told me you all were here. She also told me that Megan and Colleen planned to see a movie this afternoon—one they've already seen twice before—and that Erin and Tara were going with them, and that Shavonne would be staying in the suite with Carrie Beth and Courtney while they napped." Sissy laughed. "Then a bellboy and a desk clerk gave me your itinerary too. It wouldn't be much of an exaggeration to state that everyone on the hotel staff knows you Bradys. It's as if the hotel were a small town and the staff members are your neighbors."

Shavonne nodded. "That's the way we feel, Sissy. Everyone has been so friendly and kind to us, we feel completely at home."

She watched her attorney wipe the milk moustache from little Carrie Beth's mouth and her smile broadened. Sissy, a grandmother of three, had easily slipped into the surrogate grandma role with the two little ones. And she'd become a friend and confidant of the Brady sisters as well. Shavonne's initial impression of Sissy Timmons as a professional version of Aunt Augusta had been confirmed by the older woman's deepening involvement in their lives. All the Bradys believed implicitly that Sissy had their best interests at heart. Though she'd met Sissy only two short weeks ago, Shavonne knew she could trust her.

"Well", Sissy said warmly as she helped Carrie Beth pour ketchup on her french fries, "you've won the hearts of everyone you've met here in Houston. No one can understand how—or why—the Ramseys are behaving so shamefully toward you. Now, don't you give me that *look*, Shavonne. I'm well aware that you don't like to hear me criticize the Ramseys. I know how much you girls like Slade—why, I think the world of him myself—but his family is an entirely different story."

"Yeah, a horror story," Megan said with a smirk.

Sissy laughed heartily, and the rest of the girls joined in. Shavonne managed a small smile. She did feel uncomfortable, talking and making jokes about the Ramseys. They were, after all, Slade's family, and she knew he loved them very much. She also knew how painful his estrangement from them was for him.

Her heart had been aching for him these past two weeks. She wanted to talk to him about it, but there never seemed to be time. Though she saw Slade every day, she was never alone with him. Her sisters and nieces were always with them, and they competed fiercely for his attention. He was the first nice man in the Brady girls' lives, and they adored him.

Shavonne was grateful for his patience and understanding with her family, but she wanted some of his time and attention, too. He never sought her out, though, never tried to get her alone. Had he lost interest in her? Except as a good deed, of course.

Every night during these past two weeks, she had lain in bed and wondered what he was doing—and with whom. His visits and outings with her and her family always took place in the daytime hours. She'd heard gossip from some of the people she'd met through Sissy about the incredibly active social lives led by the younger generation of Ramseys. Was Slade spending his evenings on the town? Though he'd declared a moratorium on sex with her, there was no reason to think it extended to other women.

An intense pang of jealousy seared her. Didn't Slade want her anymore? And if he did, why didn't he end this wretched moratorium? She knew she wanted him out of bed as well as in it. How much longer would it take him to reach the same conclusion?

And suppose he never reached it? The possibility haunted her. As a caring man, he wouldn't abruptly drop all the Bradys. He'd brought them here to Houston, he felt responsible for them. If he had decided that he no longer wanted her he would doubtlessly treat her as he treated her family—like an old friend, like a sister.

He'd treat her exactly the way he'd been treating her these past two weeks.

Lunch was over and four of the Brady sisters headed for the mall's movie theater. Shavonne stuffed Courtney and Carrie Beth into their sleek new stroller and proceeded to wheel them into the passageway that joined the mall to the hotel. Sissy Timmons walked alongside her.

"I suppose Slade will be over to visit this afternoon as usual?" she asked casually, and Shavonne nodded. "Did he say what time he planned to arrive?"

"No. He said he had some business to attend to, so it would probably be later in the day. He's taken so much time off since we arrived in Houston—taking us to AstroWorld, and to the Astrodome to see our first baseball game, and to the zoo. The kids are having the time of their lives, but he isn't getting much work done."

"And what about you, Shavonne?" Sissy asked. "Are you enjoying these outings with Slade Ramsey as much as your family? Or do you wish for something . . . more with Slade?"

Shavonne felt a rush of hot color suffuse her face. She'd never told Sissy about her previous involvement with Slade; she never intended to. "What do you mean?" she asked carefully.

"Slade Ramsey is an attractive man. And he's been nothing less than heroic to champion your family's claim, despite his own family's opposition to it. Add to that the fact that he sees you every day, that he's been positively charming to you and your family . . . Well, it wouldn't be unusual for a young woman to develop a pretty serious crush on a man in such circumstances. And it wouldn't be unusual for the Ramseys to take full advantage of it."

"Honestly, Sissy, you sound almost exactly like Aunt Augusta, full of talk about Harlan's devil-kin and their devious plots."

Sissy laughed, but swiftly became serious. "It's just that I worry about you losing your head over a man who'll make you miserable, honey."

"And you think Slade will make me miserable?"

Sissy's warm blue eyes met Shavonne's. "I'll be the first to admit that Slade certainly seems to be a decent sort, the kind of reliable man that a woman can put her faith in. But—and this is a very important point, honey—Slade sets great store by his blood kin. All the Ramseys do. The Ramsey family split is the talk of Houston and the general consensus is that no one expects it to last much longer. Rumor has it that the family is looking for a way to patch things up—with everything resolved in their favor, of course. I've been tipped off that Slade plans to—" Sissy broke off abruptly.

"Plans to what?" Shavonne asked.

"You're such a dear, sweet girl. You know I've come to love you and your sisters as if . . . why, as if you were my very own nieces. Maybe that's why I seem to sound like old Aunt Augusta these days. I want what's best for all of you, and I don't want you to get hurt."

"Sissy, I'm aware of that, but I'm not going to let you weasel your way out of answering my question. You've been tipped off that Slade plans to do *what*?"

They'd reached the elevators in the hotel lobby and Sissy pressed the call button, then turned to take Shavonne's hands in hers. "My son Troy moves in the same social circles as the younger Ramseys. He happened to hear that the Ramsey family is prepared to forgive Slade and forget what they've deemed his betrayal if . . ." The older woman paused, looking distressed. "If he will make amends by marrying you and bringing your share of the mall profits back into the family coffers."

Shavonne felt the color drain from her face. Sissy squeezed her hands. "Shavonne, my dear, don't look that way! I'm just passing on what I've heard. I personally don't think that Slade will attempt any such thing. He's already proven what an ethical man he is. And I told Troy that Slade's behavior toward you has been exceptionally proper. He's been like an indulgent older brother with a pack of adoring little sisters."

"Yes," Shavonne agreed with a tight little smile. The problem was she didn't want to be his adoring little sister, she thought. But then, she didn't want to be married for her mall profits, either.

"Anyway," Sissy continued breezily, "I don't see any of the Ramsey offspring settling down and marrying for a long while yet. They all enjoy playing the field, Slade included. Why, just the other night he was seen at a party with Carling Templeton, the senator's daughter. His old girlfriend Lexie Madison was there too and having conniptions, according to the gossip mongers. Then again, who can blame Slade for wanting to get his own back with Lexie? She practically jilted him at the altar a couple years ago. Those two have the classically stormy relationship. Highly romantic, I suppose, but so exhausting."

The elevator arrived and the doors slid open. Shavonne stood motionless, the stroller in front of her, and stared into the empty car.

"Going up," Carrie Beth sang out. "Up," repeated Courtney. Shavonne still didn't move.

Sissy gave her and the stroller a gentle push inside. "Of course, if Slade should suddenly change his behavior toward you, you'll be forewarned, honey," the attorney said, patting Shavonne's shoulder. "And you know the old adage—'to be forewarned is to be forearmed.' "

She leaned down and kissed Carrie Beth and Courtney, then gave Shavonne a quick hug. "Goodbye, honey. Enjoy your visit with Slade. And don't forget. You and all the girls are coming to my house for dinner tonight. I'll have my son Troy pick you up at five-thirty here at the hotel. I'm just dying to have him meet you all!"

Shavonne nodded absently. The elevator doors closed and the car began its ascent as she stared blindly at the electronic panel. Sissy's words had struck her with the sharp force of a physical blow. She'd been hoping that Slade would stop treating her like a sister. Now she had to hope that he wouldn't. If he were to suddenly become loverlike, she would have to suspect that it wasn't because he genuinely cared for her. It would be a Ramsey family strategy to win back their lost portion of the mall.

Then there was Sissy's casual reference to Slade at a party. So he *was* spending his evenings with other women! And hearing Sissy describe his relationship with his ex-fiancée as stormy and romantic was the mental equivalent of having surgery without anesthesia. To be forewarned wasn't to be forearmed, she thought gloomily. To be forewarned was to be thoroughly miserable!

"Slade!"

At the sound of his name, Slade glanced up from the stack of papers on his desk to see his mother rushing toward him. Alice, his secretary, haplessly trailed behind her.

"I'm sorry, Mr. Ramsey," Alice said. "I told your mother that you'd given instructions not to be disturbed, but—"

"Those instructions don't apply to mothers, dear," Nola interrupted, casting the beleaguered secretary an indulgent smile. "My children are always glad to see their mama."

Slade rose from his chair. It was the first time he'd seen or spoken to his mother since the debacle

n River Oaks two weeks ago. "Hello, Mother," he
said warily.

His mother threw her arms around him. "Slade!
Do you know how much I've missed you? It's only
been two weeks and it feels like two years!"

Alice discreetly left the office, and Nola gazed up at
her son with tear-filled eyes. "I'll never be part of any
foolish feud with any of my children again. Lord, I
don't know how Harlan and Augusta stood it all
those years. Feuding with your own just isn't natural. And knowing that money is the reason for all
this shames me more than I can ever say. Tell me
you forgive me, son."

He gave his mother a swift hug. "Of course, I
forgive you, Mom."

"Oh, Slade, I've been miserable since that terrible
day!"

He nodded grimly. "So have I." The only contact
he'd had with his family these past two weeks had
been through his kid brother Ricky who'd refused to
join the rest of the Ramseys in their Slade-boycott.
"What about Dad and the others? Do they still think
I'm a curse brought down on the family by the ghost
of Great-Aunt Augusta?"

"They're as miserable as I am, son." She hugged
him again. "I admire what you did. Everyone in
Houston does. And that includes your daddy and
brothers and sister."

Slade gave a slight laugh. "Mother, you don't have
to lay it on quite so thick. I'm glad we aren't feuding
anymore. Let's leave it at that."

"We want another chance to meet those darlin'
Brady girls, Slade. To make our peace and start
over. Do you think you can bring them out to the
house for dinner tonight?" Nola's bright eyes sparkled. "We'll have an old-fashioned barbecue around
the pool. We can all get to know each other and just
have a wonderful time."

"To be perfectly honest, Mom, I don't know if they'll come." He frowned, remembering the Bradys' reaction to their initial disastrous visit to River Oaks. Poor Erin actually had become ill! And Shavonne, fiercely protective of her family, was likely to balk at subjecting them to the possibility of further emotional stress.

"But they have to come, Slade! We've heard that you see them every day. You must have some influence over them. Make them come! Granted we made a big mistake in the way we reacted to those girls, but we just can't stand by and hand them over to that conniving schemer Sissy Timmons without a fight!"

"There's no reason to fight over the Bradys, Mom. Sissy Timmons isn't a conniving schemer. She really cares about Shavonne and the girls."

Nola sniffed disdainfully. "Sissy Timmons cares about their one-quarter share of the Ramsey Park Mall. She's overly ambitious and she loves money. She'd sacrifice her own son to get it!"

"There are those who would take this opportunity to point out that Ramseys in glass houses shouldn't throw stones," Slade said dryly.

His mother scowled at him. "Don't you get smart-alecky with me, young man. I'm not just sounding off, I'm telling you the truth. Do you know Sissy's beastly son Troy? He's a junior partner in her firm and runs in the same circles as Vanessa and Jed. Well, some of his friends are predicting a match between him and the heiress."

"The heiress?" Slade stared at her. "You mean Shavonne?"

"If that's the one whose name is on the will. Slade, we can't let that happen!"

"Shavonne and Troy Timmons?" He laughed shortly. "That's ridiculous, Mother!" He began to pace the floor of his office. "They haven't even met. At least, Shavonne hasn't mentioned it to me if they have . . ."

"Does she tell you everything? I'd guess not. Especially with Sissy Timmons telling her Lord-knows-what about us!"

Shavonne and Troy Timmons? The names catapulted through his brain. Had Shavonne mentioned meeting Sissy's son? No, he knew she hadn't. Then he had a sudden thought. Hadn't Vanessa dated Troy Timmons at one time? If so, then Troy definitely wouldn't be beastly. He had to be bright, charming, and good-looking. Vanessa wouldn't even speak to a man who wasn't, let alone date one.

How would Shavonne respond if another man—a bright, charming, good-looking one—were to make a heavy play for her? Could she be swept off her feet by a new man? A man who had never hurt her? Slade clenched his fists at the painful admission. Troy Timmons wouldn't have to declare a moratorium on sex to overcome a dark past . . .

Slade frowned as he mulled over these past two weeks. He'd seen the Bradys every day but was never alone with Shavonne, and she seemed perfectly content to share him with her family. On quite a few occasions Sissy Timmons had arrived to whisk her away, leaving him with the rest of the Bradys. And though he longed to whisk Shavonne away himself, he didn't dare risk it.

He wanted her too much. Once he was alone with her, he knew what would happen. His noble intentions would be over-ridden by his love and need for her. He would do everything in his power to end their stupid moratorium on sex. And that wouldn't be fair. It was up to Shavonne to call an end to it. He was sure that would happen when she fully trusted him, when she was ready to admit she still loved him.

But it hadn't happened yet. He was beginning to wonder if it ever would.

Had this moratorium backfired on him? he wondered grimly. Sometimes he felt as if Shavonne was slipping away from him. He would find her looking at him with an odd, unreadable expression on her face, as if she were trying to assess him, as if she were waiting . . .

But for what? The next move was up to her. He believed it essential that she learn to trust him, without the complicating blindness of passion. He wanted her to come to know him as steadfast and dependable, a man she could relax and feel comfortable with.

The kind of tame and predictable man that Lexie had rejected? The thought chilled him. Had his well-intentioned actions unmanned him in Shavonne's eyes? What if nice guys simply couldn't compete with the dangerous charms of risky, elusive men? Suppose smooth Troy Timmons played it just right . . .

"If only they'd moved in with me like I'd planned!" he said. In his imagination, he'd seen Shavonne and himself swiftly resuming their relationship under his roof. Feeling alone and strange in an unfamiliar city, what could be more natural than for her to turn to him? To seek his advice, to depend on him. To realize that their moratorium on sex had served its purpose and should be put to rest.

His mother's eyes narrowed. "You planned to have the Bradys move into your house with you?"

"I thought they'd be intimidated by the hotel, and be eager to stay at my place," Slade confessed ruefully. "How was I to know the Bradys would take to hotel living like Eloise at the Plaza? And that they'd consider practically living in a mall as the greatest adventure of their lives?"

"Slade, this Shavonne Brady . . . She's more to

you than simply Augusta's heiress, isn't she?" Nola watched her son, her eyes shrewd.

"I love her," he said quietly. "I want to marry her."

"Slade!" Nola burst into smiles and threw her arms around him once more. "Oh, my darlin' boy, I'm so happy for you! I was beginning to wonder if any of my children would ever get married and make me a grandma! Your daddy is going to be over the moon when he hears this! When is the wedding? Soon, I hope!"

"You're jumping the gun, Mom. Shavonne and I haven't set a wedding date yet. I haven't even asked her to marry me." He frowned thoughtfully. "I don't know if she wants to marry me."

"Then *make* her want to." Nola grinned at her son. "You can't afford to waste a moment's time, either, honey, not with those crafty Timmonses looming on the horizon. Just remember, whatever a Ramsey wants, a Ramsey gets. That's always been our credo."

Shavonne settled Carrie Beth and Courtney in for their naps, then kicked off her shoes and sat down with a can of soda and a thick historical romance she'd bought at the book store in the mall. She paused for a moment to revel in her good fortune. All her life things like soda and books had been considered luxuries, items too expensive to purchase. A Brady drank water and borrowed books from the public library in Morgantown—if there were ever time to read, which there usually wasn't. There were always chores to be done, money to be made.

But now . . . she leaned back in the comfortable armchair and smiled. Now it was a whole new life— and she and her sisters were loving every minute of it. Little Carrie Beth and Courtney would never remember what it was like to live in poverty, and that pleased Shavonne immensely.

She'd read only a few pages when she heard a knock on the door. She jumped quickly to her feet and hurried to answer it. One thing hadn't changed in this new life: the Bradys still loved to have company and greeted visitors warmly. Sometimes members of the hotel staff, from maids to manager, dropped by to chat. They always received a gracious welcome.

"Slade!" she exclaimed happily when she opened the door. He was wearing a light gray suit and a blue shirt that emphasized the blue highlights in his slate-colored eyes. Her heart jumped. He looked incredibly attractive, masculine, sexy, and—She caught hold of herself and tried to steady her pounding pulses. "We weren't expecting you till later this afternoon. The girls have gone to the movies and—"

"You mean you're here alone?" Slade stared at the violet blouse and matching skirt she was wearing. The color was perfect for her and the soft, silky material flowed lovingly over the curves of her figure. She was wearing makeup, the expensive department-store kind. He knew because he'd been with her when the makeup consultant at Neiman-Marcus had specified which shades would be suitable for each of the sisters. Her blond hair, thick and glossy, was caught up on each side by hand-painted barrettes and fell in waves against her graceful neck.

He felt the familiar stirrings deep within him. She looked beautiful—and expensive and well-cared for. No one would guess that she'd ever had to scrimp and save, to shop at rummage sales!

She stepped aside to allow him to enter the suite. "Carrie Beth and Courtney are napping in the other room. Did I tell you that Courtney learned to climb out of the crib? We were appalled. Carrie Beth never attempted it at that age. Even now when she wants to get in the crib to play with Courtney, we still have to help her." She was babbling, her cheeks were flushed, and her smile kept wavering. What was wrong?

She was nervous, he thought. "Shavonne—" he began tentatively.

"Slade—" she said at the same time. They both lapsed into an awkward silence and stared at each other.

"You're not going to believe who stopped by my office today," he said at last.

"Carling Templeton?" she muttered under her breath. "Lexie Madison?"

He stared at her. "What did you say?"

She shrugged. "Who stopped by your office today?" she asked.

"My mother," he replied stiffly. What had she muttered to herself? he wondered. And why was she going to great lengths to avoid his eyes? Was there something she didn't want to tell him? *Or someone she wasn't telling him about?*

She brightened at the news. "Does that mean she isn't angry with you anymore?"

"Mom wants to end this stupid family feud, and she'd like to have another chance to meet you and your family." He saw Shavonne's eyes grow wary. Considering his family's behavior the last time they'd met, he could hardly blame her for having misgivings. "Please give it a chance," he added quickly. "All seven of you are invited to a barbecue in River Oaks this evening."

He'd been attending Ramsey fests all his life and knew how gracious and charming his family could be, when they chose. And tonight, he knew they would choose charm over rancor. "I promise that you'll have a wonderful time, Shavonne."

"We can't come tonight, Slade. Sissy has already invited us to dinner at her house."

He gestured impatiently with one hand. "You can call her and make it another night."

"But Sissy has already made plans to have us *tonight*. I don't think it would be fair to call and cancel now."

"She won't mind. After all, meeting my family is top priority."

Shavonne's velvety brown eyes turned cool. "I don't happen to feel that way, Slade. Why should I drop Sissy, who's been so kind and who's knocked herself out for us these past weeks, the moment your family, who's had no use for us at all, issues a summons?"

He scowled. She seemed so cool and self-possessed, so increasingly out of his reach. What had happened to his wide-eyed little country girl who looked to him for advice and approval? "I understand your feelings of loyalty toward Sissy, but—"

"I won't cancel out on Sissy. She's looking forward to tonight, she told me so. Her son is—"

"Her son?" He froze. "*Her son Troy is going to be there?*"

Shavonne took a nervous step backward. Slade looked alarmingly ferocious. As violent and as threatening as his father and brothers had looked that terrible morning in River Oaks, when they'd promised to bring misery, doom, and destruction down on the Bradys.

"No, Shavonne, I won't let this happen!" Slade thundered. "I won't let that matchmaking witch meddle in our lives!"

"Sissy isn't a matchmaking witch. She's proud of her son and wants us to meet him, that's all."

Slade knocked his palm to his forehead in a gesture of disbelief. "And if you believe that, you'll swallow anything."

"Yes, that's how you see me, isn't it? As the naive dope from Appalachia." She folded her arms across her chest and glowered at him. "The idiot who'll believe anything from 'I love you' to 'I'd like to buy your land for twenty-five thousand dollars.'"

"Are you going to throw that in my face forever? I've done everything humanly possible to make up for what's happened in the past, Shavonne."

She felt a pang of guilt. "I shouldn't've brought it up," she agreed, averting her eyes from his. "It wasn't fair. I'm very grateful for everything you've done for us, Slade. In fact, you'll always have my eternal gratitude—and my family's."

He raked her slender figure with his heated gaze. "And do you think that's what I want from you, Shavonne? Gratitude?" His voice was almost harsh.

She stared at him. The flame burning in his eyes was making her feel weak.

"Is that what you think, Shavonne?"

Her pulses skipped a beat as her eyes sought his. "Slade, I . . ." She stopped. What had she been about to say? The thought went unuttered as she lost herself in his gaze.

He reached for her and with one forceful movement pulled her into his arms. "Think again, my sweet."

Nine

Shavonne stared up at him. His pupils were dilated, darkening his eyes to a sexy, smoky gray. He lowered his gaze from her eyes to her parted lips. She felt the unmistakable heat of his arousal as he urgently pressed against her.

Her breath caught in her throat. "Slade, please. I—"

"I will, sweetheart, I'm going to please you. I can't wait to please you." And before she could think, speak, or breathe, he lowered his mouth to hers. Her lips parted on impact, automatically, instinctively, and Slade made a deep sound as his tongue probed the soft, moist warmth of her mouth.

She tried to think, but her thoughts were scattered. The taste and feel and scent of Slade filled her senses. But an inner voice, sounding suspiciously like Sissy Timmons whirled through her mind. *If Slade should suddenly change his behavior toward you . . . to be forewarned is to be forearmed . . . seen at a party with Carling Templeton . . . Lexie Madison . . . a stormy, romantic relationship . . . make amends by marrying you and bringing your share of the mall profits back into the family coffers . . .*

But that voice became muffled, then was finally mute as she felt the tremor of desire that rippled through him. His unmasked need was a potent lure, beckoning and tempting her on a most elemental level. Acting on blind impulse, she wound her arms around his neck and threaded her fingers through his thick hair.

He lifted his mouth slightly, brushing her lips with his as he spoke. "I want you so much, Shavonne. I thought I'd go out of my mind these past weeks."

She gazed up at him with cloudy, heavy-lidded eyes. "I thought you'd had plenty of company," she whispered huskily. "I heard about the party you went to the other night with Carling Templeton."

"I went to that party strictly because of business obligations. It was the first time I've gone out since you came to Houston. I've been spending my nights sitting at home thinking of you. And I went to the party without a date, Shavonne. I went alone and came home alone. I'm not interested in spending time with any woman but you."

She badly wanted to believe him, and she didn't want to waste time talking about other women. But . . . "What about Lexie Madison?" she forced herself to ask. "You two have a—a classically stormy relationship." Sissy's words echoed painfully in her head. "A highly romantic—"

"What Lexie and I had wasn't romantic, honey. It was poisonous and false and detrimental to us both. And it's over. It was over two years ago, but to drive the point home I called Lexie the day after you arrived in Houston and made sure she understood that I meant it. I want a strong and honest relationship with a woman I can trust, Shavonne. A woman who wants me for what I am and not to fulfill some immature fantasy. That woman is you, sweetheart."

She sighed. "Oh, Slade." He was saying just what she yearned to hear. She snuggled closer and a wild thrill of excitement ran through her. For a moment she clung to him, savoring the perfect fit of their bodies, softness matched to hard strength, feminine curve to masculine hollow. His hands moved slowly over her back, then his fingertips began a sensuous massage along the length of her spine.

"You're not wearing a bra," he whispered against her ear. He held her, one hand arching her against his lower body while the other covered her breast, which was soft and unfettered under her silky blouse.

"Did you deliberately decide not to wear a bra today, hoping I'd notice, Shavonne?" His voice was deep and arousing.

She shivered. Her breasts tightened, sending flames of sensual fire through her. Slade palmed the sweet curve, running his thumb lightly over the aching tip, so taut and visible through the thin material.

"Well, I noticed, sweetheart," he said with a sexy smile. "Your plan to entice me is a smashing success."

His hand slid under her blouse and moved with tantalizing slowness along her rib cage. The touch of his warm fingers on her bare skin electrified her.

"I wasn't trying to entice you," she said shakily. "At least I don't think I was."

"You don't have to be embarrassed to admit it, sweetheart. I know you always wear a bra, except those times I asked you not to. But today, I made no such request and you decided to take matters into your own hands."

It was difficult for her to think, to breathe. Liquid heat was surging through her body in swirling currents. When his hand closed over her bare breast, she uttered a small, wild cry.

He caught her nipple between his thumb and forefinger and caressed it erotically. Hot pleasure lanced her. His fingers continued their sensual play, over and over until she was moving her hips against him in a slow, provocative rhythm. "Slade," she moaned. "You don't know what you're doing to me."

"Oh, yes, love," he said softly, brushing his lips over hers. He lightly traced the outline of her full, soft mouth with the tip of his tongue. "I know exactly what I'm doing to you. Do you want me to stop?"

"No," she whispered raggedly. She was as hungry for him as he was for her. It had always been this way between them, the tides of passion surging suddenly and wildly, sweeping them both along in its wake. She stood on tiptoe and took his lower lip between her teeth in an exquisitely sensual bite.

He groaned her name and she slipped her tongue into his mouth, rubbing it seductively against his, challenging it to an erotic duel. With another deep groan, he accepted her challenge. They kissed deeply, fiercely, totally consumed with each other and the elemental storm of passion whirling through them.

He thrust his thigh between hers, and she parted her legs to cling sinuously to him. She wriggled against him, seeking more of him, yearning to fill the empty ache inside her. To fill that empty ache with him.

She whimpered as his hand slid inside the waistband of her skirt. His mouth swallowed the hungry little sound, and his hand smoothed over the silky material of her panties, kneading the provocative roundedness of her well-shaped derriere. One long finger traced along the smooth cleft, and flames of fire shot through her.

"Are you calling off the moratorium, Shavonne?" he asked hoarsely. His mouth hovered tantalizing above hers.

She wanted him so much she was dizzy from the force of it. "Are you asking me to?" she managed breathlessly.

"Only if you want to, sweet." He concentrated on nibbling on her lips.

His fingers were moving slowly, languidly, exciting her beyond measure. She took a deep breath and tossed all caution and restraint to the winds. "I want to, Slade."

The throbbing within her was becoming unbearable. She was so ready for him, her body aching, hungry, hurting for the fulfillment only he could give her.

"My darling." His voice was husky and deep, his gray eyes burning with passion.

"Now tell me that you love me," he commanded softly. "I want to hear you say the words."

"I want you so much, Slade," she cried. She wanted to make love. Here. Now. Nothing mattered, but her and Slade. Once again, there were only the two of them alone in their own private world.

She lifted her face and her mouth found his, her lips soft and seeking. She kissed him with all the emotion and intensity she was feeling, and though Slade kissed her back, she sensed his control, his deliberate withdrawal from the fiery mindlessness of their passion.

She pulled back from him and looked up into his eyes. "What's the matter?" she whispered.

"You're not going to say it, are you, Shavonne? You're not going to tell me that you love me."

She drew back farther, unnerved by the grimness of his tone. "Why are you doing this? Why are you backing me into a corner?"

He slipped his hands from beneath her clothing and released her from his arms. "I hardly think that asking you to tell me you love me is backing you into a corner, Shavonne." He stepped away from her, disappointment and frustration coursing through him.

She gazed at him suspiciously. "We aren't going to make love unless I tell you I love you?"

"No. I want you to enter into this new phase of our relationship with your eyes open." He knew he couldn't risk having her accuse him of premeditated seduction. This time they would be equal partners from the beginning.

"My eyes are wide open. I don't want to play games with you, Slade. I'm not good at them. Why can't we deal with each other openly and honestly?"

"You know that's what I want, too," he said grimly. "Believe me, Shavonne, I'm not playing games."

"Yes, you are. This is some kind of a power trip for you, isn't it? I'm supposed to tell you I love you—"

"I want you to mean it, Shavonne!"

"It's just like before." Her passion was rapidly being channeled into white-hot anger. "You make all the rules and I'm supposed to meekly obey. I have to do what you want and say what you want me to say." *If Slade should suddenly change his behavior toward you . . .* She clutched her head with her hands, as if to shut out the tormenting warning.

But her doubts could no longer be blocked. They came crashing down on her, hurting her, infuriating her. And scaring her too. She knew she was in

134 • BARBARA BOSWELL

love with Slade Ramsey and she was tempted to do anything, to say anything to belong to him again.

Even when she knew he was prepared to use her. Again.

"You love me!" he said furiously. "You're willing to go to bed with me. Hell, you're more than willing, you're downright eager!"

"That doesn't mean I'm in love with you." She lashed out at him, pain and anger making her want to hurt him, the way she was hurting. "It's like you told me two years ago. You don't have to be in love to have great sex."

Her words chilled him because he could remember saying them—on the day he had told her he was leaving and that it was all over between them. She'd cried and told him she loved him, that she knew he must love her, too. And he had said, in true rat fashion, "You don't have to be in love to have great sex."

The anger abruptly drained from him. "Somehow it seems fitting that my own words should boomerang on me," he said wryly. "Those who live by the sword die by the sword. Or, updating that to fit the eighties' social scene, if you act like a heel, you deserve to get what a heel has coming to him. Score another point for Great-Aunt Augusta's prophesy. Remember it? Time wounds all heels."

Shavonne cast a covert glance at him. He was staring at her, and she was more than a little unnerved by the intensity she saw in his piercing gray eyes. "Slade," she began uneasily.

He took both her hands in his. "It's all right, honey. I understand. I don't blame you for holding back, considering my abysmal behavior toward you the last time you told me that you loved me. You gave me a precious gift and I threw it back in your face."

Chills of apprehension tingled along her spine.

"Slade, let's not talk about it." *To be forewarned is to be forearmed . . .*

"We have to, love. I can't go on this way any longer."

"W-What way?"

"Playing the role of your pal, not touching you, not kissing you."

She made an inarticulate sound.

"Not telling you that I love you. Because I do, Shavonne. I love you and I know you love me. I want to live with you, sweetheart. I want you to be with me always." Joy flowed through him as he anticipated their future together. There would be laughter and happiness, and inevitably some quarrels and sadness, too, but everything would be buffered and buoyed by love. They would always live with love.

He pulled her closer, then carried her hands to his mouth and alternately kissed each one, gazing deeply into the depths of her eyes. "Shavonne, my love, will you marry me?"

To make amends by marrying you and bringing your share of the mall profits back into the family coffers . . . Yet even while that invidious remark flashed through her mind like a neon sign, Shavonne had to fight the temptation to say yes. She loved Slade, and she could even understand why he was doing this: family love was a powerful motivator. No one understood that better than she did at this moment. For it was because of her family that she couldn't simply cast aside common sense and practicality and risk marrying the man she loved, the man who wanted to marry her to gain control of her inheritance from Augusta Ramsey.

What would happen to her sisters, to Carrie Beth and to Courtney, if Quentin Ramsey and his sons took control of her fortune? Shavonne swallowed hard. Despite this bogus marriage proposal of his, she couldn't believe that Slade would begrudge her family financial security. Unfortunately, she also couldn't believe that Quentin, Rad, and Jed Ramsey would be willing to see the Bradys financially secure for life.

"Shavonne?" Slade asked worriedly. Her silence, her total lack of response, pierced the euphoric cloud that had so deliciously engulfed him.

He stared at her. She didn't look at all like a woman who had just received a proposal of marriage from the man she loved. She was standing tense and rigid, her usually expressive face carefully blank. And her eyes—which he'd seen burn with passion or soft with love or dancing with laughter—were devoid of any emotion.

His stomach lurched convulsively. Her lifeless eyes conveyed an alarming message, one he didn't want to believe. "Sweetheart, what is it?"

"I can't marry you, Slade," she said flatly. She tried to pull her hands from his. He refused to release her, tightening his grip instead to tug her closer.

"I won't accept that, Shavonne." Suspecting her refusal was bad enough, hearing it was absolutely intolerable. No, he decided. He would *not* accept it. "We love each other and we're going to get married. Whatever is bothering you, whatever doubts you might have . . . we'll work everything out, honey. *After* the wedding. Once we're married we'll have the time and the opportunity to—"

"One would get the distinct impression that you're in a hurry to marry me," Shavonne said lightly, though her heart was contracting with pain. If only the reason for his haste was because he was mad about her.

"I am." He jerked her against him and held her captive in his arms, her body pressed tightly against his. His eyes were brimming with sensual urgency. "And I'm going to."

"Slade, I know wh—" Her lips were suddenly cap-

tured by his, and at the feel of his kiss, so hot and
hard and incredibly familiar, her body weakened
and she shivered with dangerous delight. His tongue
probed the moist hollow of her mouth as he slowly,
seductively, rocked from side to side, rubbing his
chest against her breasts.

It was as if the disturbing interlude had never
interrupted their passion. Shavonne was instantly
hurled back to that wild moment when she'd cast all
inhibitions aside and admitted that she was calling
off their moratorium. She didn't want to think of
Slade's demand that she tell him she love him or his
heartbreakingly premeditated marriage proposal. She
didn't want to think at all.

The sensuous movement of his body against hers
made her whimper with a curious mixture of long-
ing and satisfaction. She was glad to be back in his
arms, but she wanted more than just a kiss. Much
more. She wanted to lose herself in the maelstrom of
passion that swirled between them. She wanted to
forget everyone and everything, but the two of them
and this moment, so she could freely give herself to
the man she loved without the accompanying entan-
glements of family loyalties and obligations.

"Yes, love, yes," Slade whispered, feeling her body
melt and flow like warm honey in his hands. Impa-
tient with her clothing, he placed his mouth against
the lush curve of her breast and kissed her through
the violet silk. Her nipple peaked and tingled, and
she gasped at the sensual shock wave that jolted
through her.

Her heart seemed to stop beating when his hand
moved to the top button of her blouse, then began
to race wildly as he slowly, carefully, released the
small silk-covered button from its loop.

"I was an idiot to have stopped earlier," he said
hoarsely as he unfastened each button. He sampled
the smooth, soft skin of her neck, alternately nib-

bling with his teeth and stroking with his tongue. "This is what we both want, what we both need . . ."

The blouse was open now, and he slipped it off her shoulders. "We'll talk later." After they made love. After they made love, everything would be all right, he assured himself. Shavonne, would know how much he loved her. Her hesitation to marry him would be dissolved in the fiery heat of their mutual passion.

His fingers moved to the button on her skirt, and he deftly undid it, then released the zipper. The skirt drifted to the floor to lie next to the blouse in a silky purple pile. Shavonne stood before him in her sheer panty hose and pale violet half-slip. The filmy slip accented the slender curve of her waist, the gentle flare of her lips.

"You're beautiful," he said softly, adoring her with his eyes.

She went to him, sliding her hands under his suit jacket to feel the muscular hardness of his back beneath the crisp cotton of his shirt. "You're so warm," she said throatily, reveling in the feel of him. "So strong."

His jacket joined her clothes at their feet. Boldly, she pulled his shirt from the waistband of his trousers. He drew in a sharp breath as her hands slipped under the shirt and found his bare skin. She combed through the silky hair on his chest, then dipped her thumb beneath his belt to provocatively circle his navel.

"Oh, Lord, Shavonne," he said in strangled tones. "You're making me crazy. I want to be inside you. Deep, deep . . ." His voice trailed off as she stood on tiptoe and pressed her mouth to his.

Their kiss was ardent and intense. Desire, primitive and profound, burned through them, drawing them deeper and deeper into the flame.

"Slade, I love you." She willingly gave him the

words she'd refused to parrot on demand. He was her first lover, her first and only love. And though she knew the true reason behind his sudden declaration of love and proposal of marriage, she couldn't help but hope that maybe he did care for her, somewhat. Maybe he loved her, just a little?

That would have to be enough for her, she told herself. A woman in love had to take what she could get, even if it wasn't the guaranteed happy ending of her dreams. A woman in love must suffer the consequences, either willingly or unwillingly. She'd learned that unromantic and unrelenting principle from her mother's and Erin's experiences. And Slade had taught it to her himself two years ago. She was getting another lesson today.

But she was willing, willing to love Slade, to give herself to him. The only thing she could not, would not do was to jeopardize her family's future by marrying him.

"Shavonne," he murmured, his gray eyes rapt. "Darling, I—"

"Shh!" She laid gentle fingers over his lips. "You said we'd talk later." At least the passion between them was real and honest. She didn't want it diluted or sullied with words that weren't.

"If that's what you want, sweetheart." He lifted her in his arms and carried her into the bedroom. Perhaps it was better this way, he thought. The old cliché "actions speak louder than words" hadn't become a cliché for nothing. It was tried and true. And this afternoon, he would physically show Shavonne how much he needed her, how much he loved her. Then he would reinforce his actions with the words.

He set her down beside the bed. "May I undress you?" he asked softly, caressing her thighs through the sensuous violet silk.

"If I can return the favor."

He chuckled. "It's a deal."

"Come here then," she said, grabbing his tie and pulling him to her, her dark eyes warm with sexy humor.

Slade went willingly. He loved her lack of sexual shyness with him. All the stumbling blocks and mis-understandings that seemed to plague them outside the bedroom were miraculously cast aside when they became lovers. It fueled his optimism for their future together. He was certain they could build the trust and communication necessary to make their rela-tionship as fulfilling emotionally as it was sexually. He and Shavonne were right for each other, they could make it work.

He removed her slip, and a shudder of desire coursed through him as he caressed her bare stom-ach.

"Slade," she gasped softly. He eased her down onto the bed, kissing her with a raw urgency that called forth an equally wild response from her. She felt the heat in her thighs and her abdomen and her breasts, and she clutched at him, pulling him closer.

He peeled her violet-tinted panty hose from her. His lips trailed in the wake of the hose, kissing, tasting, sending her soaring higher and higher. Then his hands were at her hips again, and her lacy pan-ties were pulled from her body, down her thighs, and off her ankles, in one deft sweep.

She lay on the bed, naked and vulnerable and passionately alive with need. "Oh, Slade, I can hardly believe this is happening," she whispered, her voice soft with emotion. "I've missed you so much. When you left me, I thought I would die from the loneli-ness, the pain. I thought I'd have to go through life without . . ."

"It's all over now, love," he murmured against her neck. "We're back together and we'll never be apart again." He kissed her, a deep, lingering kiss of lov-ing sweetness.

It wasn't time to think or to talk. Shavonne pushed his words to the back of her passion-fogged brain and gave in to her own fiery demands. Her fingers were trembling and she struggled awkwardly with his tie, until he came to her assistance. Then the two of them worked together to frantically strip away his clothes.

They kissed with wildness that sent both of them spiralling into a tempest of rapture. His fingers sought the feminine core of her as his tongue thrust deep into her mouth, in hot, smooth strokes. She felt the sweet, melting heat flow through her and began to press rhythmically against him, her hips instinctively arching to his. Her body was clamoring for his with a demanding urgency that wouldn't be denied.

When his tongue slowly withdrew, she whispered his name, her lips against his. "Love me, Slade," she pleaded achingly. "Love me now."

"Oh, sweetheart." He groaned and shifted, so that the pressure of his hard arousal was exactly where her body wanted it to be. "I intended to make it last, I wanted to take it long and slow with you . . ." He drew a deep, rasping breath. "But I don't think I can wait any longer."

"I don't want to wait." She quivered as she felt his hands slide under her hips to position her to receive him. Her eyes snapped closed and she clutched his shoulders, her lilac-pink polished nails sinking into his damp, heated skin.

Her implicit surrender broke the last vestiges of his control, and he drove into her, filling her with one powerful stroke. She felt a moan escape from her throat as her body enveloped him.

"Look at me," he said hoarsely, and she gazed up into the hot, gray eyes of her lover.

For a moment, they were motionless as they stared

at each other silently acknowledging the strength and depth of their intimacy.

And then the familiar and incredible pleasure of their joining swept through them both. Shavonne uttered a soft sigh and clung to him, tightening the small muscles within her as he had taught her to do, pleasing herself as she pleased him.

It was a frantic mating. There was no time or need for smooth technique or finesse, only a driving urge to take and give the profound joy they'd always found together. They moved as one, their fusion more sublime, more meaningful than ever before because of their long and painful separation.

This was so much more than sex, Shavonne thought in those last seconds before all thoughts were blurred. This was truly a union, and not only a physical one. She felt emotionally untied with him; two minds and souls and bodies that had met and merged perfectly. "Slade, oh, Slade," she whispered imploringly. He was hers; she would never let him go.

He whispered to her, erotic and intimate words that fanned the incandescent flames burning within her to an even greater intensity. His sexy voice was as arousing as his hands and his body, and she gloried in his possession and her own surrender.

She cried his name again and again as he moved masterfully inside her. And then the wild and heavenly pleasure, volcanic in its force, erupted within her and sent her spinning into a mindless realm of ecstasy.

The luscious pulses of her body triggered Slade's own completion. Lost in love, she held him tightly as she felt his life-force surge into her with exultant power. This was what she'd been dreaming of since the day he had left her, she thought as tears of joy filled her eyes. She and Slade together, loving, giving, taking. She trembled with the force of her emotions. *Slade, Slade, we're so good together*, she cried soundlessly. *So good . . .*

Shavonne wasn't sure how long she drifted in the warm seas of sexual satiation before she slowly, reluctantly began to surface. She opened her eyes to meet Slade's intent gaze. He smiled and stroked her hair away from her forehead with gentle hands.

"I love you," he said in a voice husky with emotion.

Her eyes filled with hot tears, which she swiftly blinked away. "Slade, please don't."

"I have to say it. Don't ask me to lock what I'm feeling for you inside me. I want to shout it to the world—Slade Ramsey loves Shavonne Brady. And she loves him." He bent his head to touch his lips to hers. "Doesn't she?"

She framed his face with her hands. "Yes," she whispered. "Oh, yes, Slade. I've never stopped loving you. I think you realized that before I did."

He smiled a smile of lazy satisfaction. "Well, now that you mention it . . ."

She rolled her eyes and playfully tweaked his nose. "Smug, arrogant male."

With one swift movement, he rolled her on top of him and held her there. "And I'm all yours."

"You'd better not forget it," she warned with mock severity.

They both laughed, and she wriggled sensuously, enjoying the seductive freedom this position allowed her. She was enjoying Slade's playful teasing, too. This was the first time they'd ever indulged in lightness and humor after loving. During their affair, their intense and passionate sex had been taken very, very seriously. Yet their lovemaking this afternoon had been just as intense and passionate as before.

She gazed at Slade lovingly. She felt so close to

him, more connected to him than she'd ever felt before. Was he feeling this newfound intimacy, too? Could this warm closeness between them be the reason why they could relax so completely with each other?

His hands caressed her back, from the sensitive hollow at the base of her spine to the nape of her neck. "When are you going to marry me, sweet?" he murmured huskily.

She came back to earth with an unpleasant, figurative thud. So they were back to that again? She suppressed a sigh, as the unseen Bradys and Ramseys made their presence very much felt here in her and Slade's private world. "Slade, I—I don't want to get married," she managed to say, and tensed, bracing herself for the inevitable explosion.

It didn't come. There was a moment's silence, then he shifted their positions so that she was lying alongside him, tucked into the curve of his body. He tilted her chin with his fingers and made her meet his eyes. "Why don't you want to get married, honey?"

He sounded so understanding, so reasonable. She was tempted to blurt out the truth, to tell him that she couldn't consider marrying him because she didn't trust his family with her fortune, and her fortune was *her* family's future.

But she didn't dare tell him *that*! She snapped out of her love-induced languor almost at once. She loved him so much, but he was a Ramsey and a man, and she didn't fully understand or trust either Ramseys or men. Images of her four sisters and her two nieces passed through her head in filmstrip fashion, reminding her of where her love and loyalties must lie.

"I'm not ready to get married," she said at last. "I—I want to finish my education, get my degree."

"I think that's a wonderful idea," he said enthusiastically. "You can transfer your credits from WVU to a school here. There's no reason why you can't complete your studies as a married student. In fact, I'll do everything in my power to help you." He paused to kiss her deeply, arousingly. "And I promise I won't use tactics like this to keep you from studying when you have an exam or a paper due."

For a moment, she allowed herself to imagine her life as Slade's wife. A married woman attending college classes, returning to her home and husband at the end of each day. It seemed like a lovely dream. And a dream was exactly what it had to remain, she reminded herself sternly.

"I just don't want to get married," she lied, hoping she sounded forceful enough. "I . . . uh . . . uh . . . I'm too young. I don't want to settle down for years and years. You'll just have to accept that. I don't want to keep arguing with you about it."

He stared at her for a long moment. She looked away, unable to endure the piercing sharpness of his shrewd eyes. "You said you love me," he said quietly. "And I believe that you do, Shavonne. After what we just shared . . ."

"I do love you!" she hastened to reassure him.

"But you don't want to marry me."

She shook her head, gazing down at him sadly. She thought she saw something flicker in his eyes, but it was gone so quickly that she wasn't sure. "I hope you understand," she murmured weakly.

"Oh, I think I do." He flashed a smile that wasn't really a smile at all. More of a grimace, she thought nervously, although that wasn't quite it, either. Was there a specific word for what a wolf did when it bared its teeth?

"Okay, Shavonne, we'll do it your way." His voice was calm and controlled. Pleasant in a deadly sort of way. "We'll have another affair."

Did he think she would back down at the bald statement? she wondered. Well, she would surprise him. "Yes," she said. "Let's have an affair." She couldn't marry him, but she couldn't give him up, either. She was quite accustomed to sacrifice and compromise; she'd learned early to adjust her wants and needs to fit reality. She did it now, without thinking to protest the unfairness of it all.

"All right." He nodded his agreement. "An affair it is." Actually, Slade was feeling relieved. When she'd turned down his proposal, he had been sickeningly certain that she would insist on completely ending it between them.

"But don't expect this to be a lukewarm sort of affair," he continued, his voice lowering seductively. He moved swiftly on top of her, pinning her beneath him. "It's going to be very hot, very passionate, very intense." His eyes glittered as he parted her legs with his thigh. "And very sexual. The moratorium has ended forever. From now on, we're going to be very sexual with each other."

His hand slipped between them and he found her ready for him. She blushed a little at the unquestionable evidence of her desire.

"You want me again." He was stating an obvious fact, not asking, and she closed her eyes and gave a swift little nod. "Now,' he said, and she nodded again.

She opened herself to him and he surged into her, filling her once more, making her moan with satisfaction. "I was afraid you'd be so angry that you wouldn't want me anymore," she confided breathlessly as she wrapped herself around him. "I thought if I wouldn't marry you, you'd tell me it was all over."

"No, honey," he said soothingly. "If an affair is what you want, then that's what we'll have. I won't bother you with any more tiresome proposals of marriage. You don't have to worry about me mentioning the word marriage again."

"When you say it like that it sounds so—so cold and hard. That's not how I want it to be, Slade."

"I know, lover, you want it hot and hard." He

laughed at his double entendre. "Like this." The sensual rhythm of his movements sent flames of liquid fire to her every nerve.

Her heart was hammering wildly. She was excited and writhing with need and totally confused by the mixture of emotions Slade stirred within her. She wanted to laugh and cry at the same time.

"Put it all out of your mind, honey," he commanded softly. "Everything that's worrying you, anything that's bothering you. Forget it all and let me take care of you."

She started, stunned by his perception. "I want to, Slade."

"Then come to me, darling." He covered her mouth with his own and she allowed herself to empty her mind of everything but Slade and their love.

Their bodies held and moved as one. The room was filled with soft sighs and whispered words and the erotic sounds of lovers making love. Together Shavonne and Slade scaled the heights of rapturous abandon, and together they found transcendent peace as their passion exploded into blissful release.

Ten

When her four sisters trooped into the hotel room, laughing and talking about the movie they'd seen, Shavonne was serving Carrie Beth and Courtney a postnap snack of cookies, milk, and fruit. Slade sat at the table, too, entertaining the children by making the pieces of apple talk to the cookies.

"How come you changed clothes, Shavonne?" Megan asked, eyeing her eldest sister's butter-yellow jumpsuit curiously. "I thought you were wearing your new violet outfit to Sissy's tonight."

Shavonne glanced away as she recalled the hopelessly wrinkled state of those garments when she'd retrieved them from the floor a little less than an hour ago. Slade's clothes weren't in much better condition. He looked distinctly rumpled in his blue shirt and gray slacks. His jacket and tie lay in a discarded heap on the chair.

Her eyes flickered to his and met and held his gaze. He smiled at her, and her heart clenched. His hair was tousled and his expression was one of relaxed satiation. She inhaled sharply as sensual memories of their afternoon together washed over her. It was incredibly satisfying to know that she was responsible for Slade's air of contentment. As he was for hers.

She smiled back at him and unspoken messages passed between them. They were having an affair, she thought, and her blood heated. A very passionate, very intense, very sexual affair. Erin sat down at the table with her daughters and turned to Slade.

"Did Shavonne tell you that we called the mothers of our day nursery children this morning to tell them we wouldn't be back to reopen?"

He glanced sharply at Shavonne. "No, she must have . . . forgotten to mention it to me."

"We're never going back to Star City!" Colleen exclaimed exuberantly. "Last night we all voted to stay here. Houston is our home now."

"Sissy said she'd arrange for our things to be shipped down from West Virginia and for both our house and Aunt Augusta's to be sold," Tara chimed in.

"Sissy said she'd arrange it?" Slade echoed. He knew it was absurd, but he felt left out. He didn't want the Bradys making plans or depending on anyone else but him. His jealousy surprised him. He'd handpicked Sissy Timmons himself, knowing how thorough and reliable she was. He'd wanted that kind of attorney for the Bradys. And yet . . .

His eyes sought Shavonne's and a fierce wave of possessiveness surged through him. "I'd assumed you'd be staying permanently in Houston," he said, rising from the table. He hooked an arm around Shavonne's waist and pulled her down beside him on the flowered sofa. "I also assumed I'd be the first one to know your plans."

"I was going to tell you when you came to visit today," Shavonne said, "but we . . . um, we started talking about other things after you arrived. Remember?"

A sexy smile spread slowly across his face. "Oh, I

remember very well." His eyes told her that he was remembering everything about their passionate afternoon.

She squirmed. If they'd been alone, she would have climbed onto his lap and subjected him to the most exquisite sensual punishment for teasing her. But her family was very much present. Within seconds, Carrie Beth was hopping up on the two of them with a storybook. Courtney followed a moment later, crawling over them, an oatmeal cookie crumbling in her little hand.

"Later," Slade murmured to Shavonne. Her mouth curved into a little smile. "Later," she agreed softly.

Slade spent the remainder of the afternoon with the Bradys. He talked to Shavonne's sisters and played with her nieces just as he'd been doing since their arrival in Houston. But his treatment of Shavonne was definitely different.

No longer did he assume the role of big brother with her. He treated her like his lover. He murmured private little asides to her, his gaze lingered upon her, he touched her frequently—slipping an arm around her or lacing her fingers with his. Occasionally, he lifted her hand to his mouth and kissed it, or brushed her lips lightly with his.

Carrie Beth and Courtney were oblivious to these intimate exchanges, but Shavonne's four sisters observed them all with watchful eyes. When Shavonne left the suite to get some ice from the machine down the hall, Tara turned to Slade and asked bluntly, "Are you and Shavonne back together?"

He shrugged. "I suppose we are . . . in a way."

"And what way is that?" Erin asked.

"I asked her to marry me and she said no." He smiled. "But that doesn't mean I'm going to stop trying to make her say yes."

"She said no?" asked Megan aghast. "But why? It would be terrific if you married Shavonne. We all like you so much—and I know Shavonne likes you, too."

"Shavonne loves me," he corrected her gently. "But she won't admit she wants to marry me . . . yet."

Colleen frowned. "Uh-oh, I think I know why."

"You do?" He turned to her with interest.

"She's playing hard to get." Colleen looked troubled. "How long are you supposed to keep it up, anyway? Did Aunt Augusta ever say when to stop?"

"You play forever," Tara said grimly. "A man always wants what he can't have."

It was Slade's turn to look grim. "Is that another gem of wisdom from my sainted aunt?"

"From Mama," Megan said.

"I hope you don't really believe that," he said quietly. He found it depressing that the three teenaged Bradys, having had so little contact with the opposite sex, should have such a warped view of men. It was even more dispiriting that Shavonne and Erin, raised on that same philosophy, had managed to find men who'd confirmed it for them.

"Of course we believe it," Colleen blithely assured him.

"But it's not true." He drew a deep breath. "It's a gross generalization that can apply to either sex—or *not* apply to either. I don't want what I think I can't have. I want to marry your sister because I love her. And if she turned down my proposal because she's playing hard to get . . ."

Tara shrugged. "It obviously worked, didn't it? Last time she didn't play hard to get and you didn't propose. You left. This time she did and, bingo, you decide you want to marry her."

He frowned. Such an incredibly stupid reason for Shavonne's refusal hadn't occurred to him. He'd thought perhaps she was still wary of him, still didn't trust him completely. He'd even wondered if she was worried about marrying a Ramsey. He was under no illusions about the impressions she'd formed of his family.

Any of those reasons, doubts, and fears he could understand and accept. He'd even intended to talk it all out with her when she felt comfortable enough with him to do so. But if she was deliberately playing games . . .

Slade felt his irritation rise. He was sick to death of games and roles and sexual manipulations. It was if he'd been spinning on a roulette wheel since Lexie's desertion and he'd felt nothing but relief when he'd called a permanent end to it all.

His relationship with Shavonne held so much promise. She was sweet, refreshingly frank, and devoid of guile. At least, he *thought* she was. Had he been all wrong about her? Was she as caught up in the intricate moves of romantic strategy as Lexie Madison?

He was still pondering all of this when Shavonne returned a few moments later with a container of ice and a smiling, handsome young man who bore a marked resemblance to Sissy Timmons. "This is Troy Timmons," she told her sisters, her dark eyes warm with laughter. "We literally ran into each other in the hall."

Troy grinned. "And I immediately recognized you as one of the Brady girls from my mother's rapt descriptions of you all. You Bradys are all she talks about these days. I just don't know which sister you are."

"Shavonne," she said, then introduced each of the others. She paused when she came to Slade. "And this is Slade Ramsey."

Troy came forward to shake Slade's hand as Slade stood up. "I know Jed and Vanessa," he said cheerfully. "And I've heard a lot about you from them, Slade. Pleased to finally meet you."

Slade gripped the younger man's hand with bone-crunching strength. He remembered his mother's warning. So this was the joker who was entertaining hopes of marrying "the heiress"? In his current mood, the timing for this meeting couldn't have been worse.

"I understand you're having dinner with the Bradys tonight," he said a bit too heartily. He was aware that his jovial tone was as patently false as his smile, but he didn't care. "Well, there's been a slight change in plans. The other six will join you, but Shavonne will be spending this evening with me. Please give her regrets to your mother."

"Slade," Shavonne said. "I told you I was going to Sissy's, too."

"No." He dropped Troy's hand and moved directly in front of her. "You're not."

An ominous silence fell over the room.

"We'll explain to Sissy," Megan said in a nervous little voice. "Go on your date with Slade, Shavonne."

"I don't have a date with Slade and I'm going to Sissy's." Shavonne forced herself to meet Slade's eyes. It took some effort. He looked so big and strong and male—and angry. But she wouldn't let him bully her out of going to Sissy's. The older woman was a good friend and Shavonne had promised she'd be there tonight.

Slade saw the determination in Shavonne's eyes. So she was *playing hard to get?* He seethed as the phrase burned into his brain. If his anger was fueled by knowledge of her deceitful little game, it was stoked even higher by the presence of Troy Timmons, who was young and handsome and amiable and—if Nola Ramsey was to be believed—had designs on Shavonne and her fortune.

"Oh, but we do have a date, darling," he said through clenched teeth. This was it. Even nice guys had their limits, and he'd just crossed his. Impetuously, he scooped Shavonne up in his arms and strode to the door. "We'll see you later, kids," he called over his shoulder as he headed out into the hall.

"Slade, put me down!" Shavonne demanded, struggling to break free. His arms seemed to be made of steel and she felt as if she were caught in a vise. Though she twisted and fought the whole way down the hall, her attempts to escape were futile.

"Let me go!" she cried furiously. "I won't stand for these caveman tactics. If you don't put me down this minute, I'll—I'll scream!"

They reached the elevators and he punched the call button. "Go ahead and scream," he said coolly, calling her bluff. He knew she wouldn't scream, of course. She would be too embarrassed to make such a scene.

Which she was. After all, it wasn't as if she were being abducted by a loathsome stranger. She'd spent the afternoon in bed with Slade, and she knew he would never harm her. Still, that didn't lessen her anger. "I won't let you manhandle me this way, Slade Ramsey!" she stormed.

The elevator arrived and the doors opened. The car was half-filled with passengers. She saw their amused and curious stares and turned her head into Slade's shoulder with a mortified groan.

Grinning bellhops and desk clerks called their good-byes as Slade carried her through the lobby. The doorman had Slade's car brought around while he chatted deferentially with "Mr. Ramsey, sir," seemingly oblivious to the smoldering Shavonne held fast in Mr. Ramsey's arms.

Slade dumped her into the front seat of his midnight-blue Maserati. "Don't even think of trying to run for it while I'm getting into the car," he warned. "Because I promise I'll chase you—and I'll catch you. And we both know, it, don't we, darling?"

"Stop saying 'darling' in that condescending tone,"

she ordered with a glare. He slammed the car door shut, and she toyed with the idea of leaping out and making a break for the elevators. But Slade was watching her as he walked around the front of the car, and she had no doubt that he would do exactly what he'd threatened. He'd just proven that he didn't care if he made a public spectacle of himself—and her!

"Where are we going?" she asked crossly as he climbed into the seat.

He clicked his safety belt shut and turned the key in the ignition. "You'll find out when we get there."

The Maserati was a far cry from the rented van Slade normally drove to squire the Bradys on their various outings. It was the type of sleek, sexy car that a rich, sophisticated bachelor would drive. She sank her teeth into her lower lip and fought against feeling intimidated.

They sped along the highway in complete silence. Shavonne felt herself growing more and more nervous. To what lengths would Slade and the Ramseys go to get back full control of their mall?

She knew she had to distract herself from her increasing anxiety. "Do you mind if I turn on the radio?" she asked, hoping to sound cool and nonchalant, as if being abducted from a hotel room was a commonplace occurrence in her life. She glanced at the unrelenting set of Slade's jaw and gulped. Music, news, a call-in talk show—anything—had to be preferable to this thoroughly unnerving silence.

"Be my guest," he said with exaggerated politeness, then added mockingly, "Scared, Shavonne?"

Shavonne, who had been leaning forward to switch on the dial, abruptly sat back in her seat. "Scared of you?" She affected a scornful laugh. "No, I'm not afraid. I'm outraged!"

"Well, so am I, baby, so am I."

She stared at him, nonplussed. "Why are you outraged?" she asked, her curiosity getting the better of her.

"I told you that I wanted a strong and honest relationship with a woman I can trust. I've had it with game-playing man-eaters. If that's what you want to be—"

"A game-playing man-eater?" she repeated, astonished. "*Me?*"

He cast a quick glance at her and scowled. "I didn't mean it as a compliment, Shavonne."

"Well, I'm taking it as one. I've always considered myself singularly backward when it came to dealing with men. But game-playing man-eaters are pros. And if a hot-shot bachelor like you thinks that I've—"

"I'm not a hot-shot bachelor and you know it. Rad and Jed are hot-shot bachelors. And Troy Timmons. I'm a nice guy who wants to settle down with the woman I love. I want to have kids." A sly smile suddenly lit his face. "And I may have one sooner rather than later. We didn't use any protection this afternoon, did we, sweetheart?"

She gasped. "I forgot all about it!"

"So did I, for the first time ever. My practical, cautious self dissolved the moment I took you into my arms."

Shavonne was doing some frantic mental calculations. "I doubt I'll get pregnant," she informed him breathlessly. "It's the wrong time of the month."

He arched his brows. "Are you as sorry about that as I am? And as determined to try again during the right time of the month?"

A syrupy warmth flowed through her. "I adore Carrie Beth and Courtney," she said huskily. "I've always wanted a little girl of my own, just like them."

"What about a gray-eyed, dark-haired bouncing baby boy?"

"No, thank you," she said sweetly. "Heaven only knows what kind of damage a game-playing man-eater like me could wreak on a defenseless male infant."

Slade tried and failed to suppress a grin. "That's not fair, Shavonne," he complained. "How am I supposed to stay infuriated if you make me laugh?"

"Maybe you could stop being infuriated," she suggested tentatively. "Maybe we both could."

"Maybe. Will you stop playing games and marry me?"

She laid her head against the back of the seat and stared through the windshield. "I thought you weren't going to bother with any more tiresome proposals of marriage," she said lightly, and swiftly added, "That was a direct quote from you, remember?"

"I remember." He tightened his grip on the steering wheel until his knuckles were white, but his tone matched hers in lightness when he said, "Still not ready to call it quits, hmm?"

In his head, he heard young Colleen's voice ask plaintively, *"How long are you supposed to keep it up, anyway? Did Aunt Augusta ever say when to stop?"* And then Tara had replied, *"You play forever. A man always wants what he can't have."* The Bradys had been raised on this tripe, he reminded himself in an effort to ease his impatience, and he'd certainly contributed to its veracity in their eyes.

"I'm taking you to my parents' home in River Oaks," he said, his tone decisive and firm. "The whole family will be there, and they're prepared to make amends for what's happened. I hope you'll give them another chance, Shavonne."

Her stomach gave a convulsive lurch. "Do they know that you asked me to marry you?"

He remembered his little chat with his mother and her words of maternal wisdom. *Whatever a Ramsey wants, a Ramsey gets.* "I suppose they do," he confessed wryly. Since he'd stated his inten-

tions, the Ramseys would consider the marriage a
fait accompli.

Of course they would know, Shavonne thought
glumly. They'd probably worked out the plan at a
family summit meeting. She had a mental picture of
such a meeting, Quentin Ramsey presiding. First on
the agenda: getting back the mall.

Oh, Slade, her heart cried, *if only you'd be honest with me.*

It was a subdued couple who arrived at the River
Oaks mansion where Quentin and Nola greeted them
like visiting royalty. As Slade had warned, the whole
family was there, his parents and Ricky, Vanessa,
Jed, and Rad.

If Shavonne had thought the Ramseys were overwhelming when angered, she decided that they were
twice as overpowering when welcoming a prospec-
tive member to the fold. The Ramseys assumed she
was marrying Slade and gave her no opportunity to
state otherwise.

"Let's have the wedding as soon as possible," Quentin boomed. "Why waste time when it's something
we all want so much?"

Why indeed? Shavonne asked herself dryly. She
wouldn't have been surprised if he'd produced a
justice of the peace to perform the ceremony then
and there—along with an attorney and a deed for
her to sign. A deed that handed her portion of the
Ramsey Park Mall back to the Ramseys.

To their credit, the Ramseys weren't quite that
blatant. But they certainly went out of their way to
bludgeon her with charm. Their keen interest in her
every answer to the hundreds of questions they fired
at her, their five thousand-watt smiles that would
have dissolved a lesser candidate into a puddle of
nerves . . .

The dogged conviviality of the Ramseys made her
think of a basketful of cobras, determined to con-

vince their intended prey that they were merely a harmless bunch of friendly, neighborhood garter snakes. But Shavonne wasn't cowed. She'd faced smiling faces far more intimidating than the Ramseys. The smiling judge who'd wanted to place her sisters in foster homes after the unexpected death of their mother from complications of hepatitis. The smiling representatives of the various utilities who'd threatened to cut off service to the Brady home due to the family's inability to meet the monthly payments . . .

She'd been penniless and powerless back in those days, but she had held her own with them all, convincing each that she could cope, could handle responsibility, would pay what they could. In her family's presence, she was at her most vulnerable because she worried about their reactions, but alone with her opposition, Shavonne held firm, supported by her own inner strength.

And she had Slade's support. She was pleasantly surprised by that. If he thought his family's questions were becoming too personal or painful, he interceded on her behalf. He didn't once try to force the issue of marriage, which would have been easy for him to do considering his family's overwhelming enthusiasm for it. He acted like her friend and ally, not like her lover, and she was grateful for that. She wasn't sure what she would have done if he had insisted on showy displays of affection in front of his over-eager relatives. The warm smiles he gave her, the occasional times he squeezed her hand— those small gestures were more real and more meaningful to her than any overblown caresses he might have made to cement his claim in front of his family.

No one mentioned the land or the mall or Augusta Ramsey. Not until dinner was over and they were all gathered on the spacious screened-in porch with iced after-dinner drinks was anything remotely connected with finance brought up.

And then Quentin said ever-so-casually, "Of course, after you're married to Slade, you'll want different legal counsel to handle your financial affairs, Shavonne, my dear. May I suggest Ramsey and Sons' personal attorney, J. D. Haynes? He has the shrewdest legal mind in Texas and—"

"I'm quite satisfied with my current attorney, Mr. Ram—uh, Quentin," Shavonne said. It felt unnatural to call Slade's parents by their first names, but they'd insisted, at least fifty times during the course of the evening. She would concede on that point, but on giving up Sissy Timmons—never.

"Shavonne is quite loyal to Sissy, Dad," Slade added, and Shavonne saw the warning glance he cast to his father.

Quentin saw it too. "Loyalty is an admirable quality," he said, turning back to Shavonne with a smile so brilliant she had to blink. "You've won yourself a precious girl, son. I'll be pleased when the day comes and she transfers that loyalty to us Ramseys."

"Along with her deed to the mall," Jed muttered to Ricky under his breath. No one heard, not even Ricky, because Jed had spoken so quietly.

Shavonne happened to read his lips, though. It wasn't hard, since she'd had the same thought he'd voiced. She reminded herself once again that tonight was all a charade. The Ramseys didn't adore her as they were pretending to do. Quentin Ramsey didn't think his son had found a precious girl, but a nuisance who had to be stopped at any cost. And Slade was willing to pay the ultimate price—marriage to her—to keep peace and the Ramsey Park Mall intact in his family.

The adrenaline high that had carried her through the tensions of the evening abruptly ended, and her spirits plummeted hard and fast. She wished she were with her family, where she could relax this constant guard. Her face hurt from smiling, and she wondered what would happen if she dared not to smile anymore. How did the Ramseys keep it up? she wondered wearily. Laughing, talking, smiling, when they didn't want her here any more than she wanted to be here?

She happened to glance at Slade and found him watching her. He'd been watching her all evening. This time he didn't smile when her eyes met his. He leaned forward in his seat and held her gaze, as if trying to draw her out of herself and into him, as if—

"Excuse me, sir."

Shavonne jumped as the voice of the Mexican maid pierced the compelling aura of Slade's stare. It was strange, but for those brief moments, she and Slade had been so psychically attuned that she'd actually blocked out everyone and everything but him. Feeling slightly disoriented, she glanced around to see the Ramseys turn their attention to the uniformed young woman, who was looking none too happy.

"Yes, Dolores, what is it?" Nola asked.

"Miss Lexie Madison is here," Dolores said rather nervously. "I told her that the family was entertaining a dinner guest, but she refused to leave."

A stunned silence fell over the terrace. After the initial shock passed, Shavonne found herself watching the Ramseys, feeling curiously detached from the entire scene. Slade was frowning, his eyes narrowed. Vanessa looked irked, Ricky disbelieving, Rad amazed. Jed, Quentin, and Nola seemed to be taking it the worst. They appeared positively aghast.

Quentin recovered first. "Dolores, tell her that—" But he didn't have a chance to finish his instructions to the maid for a beautiful, tall redhead joined them on the terrace.

"Lexie," Ricky said with a groan. All the Ramseys were staring at the woman as if they'd never seen her before.

Shavonne gazed covertly at Lexie Madison but did not permit herself to gape. She took in Lexie's cover-girl features and glorious, burnished mane of hair, the ultra-trendy, sexy, champagne-colored dress and—Shavonne blinked—the excitement glowing in the other woman's dark blue eyes. That struck her as strange. She could have understood heartbreak, fear, anger or desperation, but excitement?

"Lexie, what are you doing here?" Slade asked, his voice deep and low. He was sitting beside Shavonne on a padded chaise longue and he inched a little closer to her.

"Vanessa told me you were having . . . company tonight," Lexie said in a throaty voice.

Every pair of Ramsey eyes shifted accusingly toward Vanessa. "I didn't invite her over," Vanessa exclaimed righteously. "I just happened to mention that Slade's . . . uh, new fiancée was coming for dinner,"

Shavonne noted that the Ramseys' collective anxiety was almost palpable now. The cobras thought they'd convinced the golden goose that they were harmless and along came an intruder who threatened to unmask them. The fanciful absurdity almost made her giggle, although she supposed the Ramseys found no humor in the situation.

Actually, they were glowering at Lexie, reminding Shavonne of the reception she and her family had been treated to earlier. At least she now knew it hadn't been personal, she mused dryly. Anyone standing in the way of the Ramseys' acquisition of their missing portion of the mall was accorded the same treatment. Since Lexie Madison had become the obstacle that Shavonne herself had originally represented, the full force of the Ramsey ire was turned upon her.

Nola sprang to her feet and came to stand beside Shavonne. "Lexie, I'm proud to introduce you to the sweet, wonderful girl that our Slade is going to marry." The older woman lay a protective hand on Shavonne's shoulder. "Shavonne, darlin', this is Lexie Madison, an old school chum of Vanessa's."

"Mother, Shavonne knows that Lexie and I were once engaged," Slade said wearily. He looked at Shavonne, but she kept her expression carefully polite.

"They broke up eons ago," Rad added hastily.

"Yes, Miss Madison is just a bit of Ramsey ancient history," Quentin seconded, joining his wife beside Shavonne.

Lexie made a small sound. She looked stricken by the Ramseys' mass defection, Shavonne thought. The excitement in her blue eyes had been replaced by hurt, and Shavonne felt a shaft of sympathy for her. It must be painful for Lexie to be so frankly disavowed by the family she'd once been welcomed to join.

"Slade, may I speak to you for a few minutes?" Lexie asked in a tremulous voice.

Slade grimaced. "Lexie, we really don't have anything to say to each other," he said coolly.

Shavonne's eyes flicked from Slade to Lexie and back to Slade again. As far as she could tell, he didn't look moved by his former fiancée's pain or tearful beauty. In fact, he looked . . . exasperated?

"Slade, please—" Lexie began, but Quentin cut her off with a hearty, "Young lady, Slade is otherwise occupied, as you can see for yourself. Vanessa, see Miss Madison to the door." He cast his daughter a baleful glare. "Immediately."

Shavonne would bet that that particular look and tone of Quentin Ramsey's had sent many jumping to do his bidding, but his daughter seemed completely immune. With deliberate slowness, she got to her feet, stretched, then strolled indolently toward

Lexie. There was complete silence as everyone watched the two women leave the terrace.

Then the Ramseys all began to talk at once, each one of them apologizing profusely for Lexie's untimely appearance and offering reassurances of Slade's total lack of interest in the woman. All the Ramseys except for Slade, Shavonne noticed. He sat silently beside her, listening to his family, his elbows resting on his knees as he held his head in his hands.

The screened-in walls seemed to be closing in on her. She needed space, silence. She needed to be away from the Ramseys' indomitable presence. "Will you excuse me for a few moments?" she asked, rising swiftly to her feet. "I'd like to use the powder room."

For a moment, she thought they were going to refuse to let her go and actually keep her captive there on the porch. But they must have realized that wouldn't be seemly, so Nola and Quentin nodded and Rad and Jed stood aside to let her pass.

She had already been shown the turquoise and silver powder room earlier in the evening, but she had no luck locating it again. She wandered along the hall and made a hopeful turn, thinking how incredible it was to actually be lost in someone's home. One got lost in museums or hotels or shopping malls, but in a house?

She paused, debating on whether to turn left or make another right when she heard Vanessa Ramsey's voice. She reacted instinctively. She flattened herself against the wall and didn't make a sound.

"For heaven sake's, Lexie, don't you have any sense at all?" Vanessa's irritated voice carried clearly down the corridor. "I can't believe you'd go so far as to show up tonight and try to mess things up for us!"

Shavonne bit her lip and wondered if she should

make her presence known, or try to slip away undetected, or—

"Vanessa, Slade is going to marry that girl! I can't let that happen!" Lexie's anguished wail froze Shavonne in place. As much as she didn't want to hear this, as guilty as she felt about eavesdropping, she couldn't tear herself away from her secret listening post.

"You know how much I want him back!" Lexie exclaimed, and though pain ripped through her, Shavonne felt an odd kinship with Slade's former fiancée. She remembered all too well her own terrible hurt at losing Slade.

"I know you didn't want him when you had him," Vanessa snapped. "Let's not kid ourselves, Lexie. You only started wanting Slade when you knew you couldn't have him. Anyway, Slade's never considered asking you to marry him again and you know it. That's what kept you interested in him—the challenge. And that has nothing to do with love."

Shavonne thought about that. Her mother had believed that only men wanted what they couldn't have, and yet according to Vanessa, Lexie Madison was governed by the same motive. But Slade wasn't, Shavonne realized. Lexie was nothing like Slade. She herself understood Slade in a way that the drama-loving redhead never would.

"Vanessa, you said you agreed with me for breaking it off with Slade!" Lexie's voice had risen sharply. "You've steered clear of the steadfast, marrying kind yourself. But, oh, Vanessa, since we broke up Slade has been anything but steadfast. He's exciting—"

"Elusive, a little bit cruel," Vanessa cut in with typical Ramsey bluntness. "Just your kind of guy, Lexie. The problem is that Slade hasn't been himself. He's been acting a role, and one that doesn't suit him. And I said I *understood* why you broke it off, but that doesn't mean I liked it—or liked you for doing it. Slade's my brother and you made him miserable. You've tried to make him into something he isn't."

"Don't tell me you think that little blond baby doll he's with now will make him happy," Lexie said.

"Maybe she will," Vanessa replied coldly. "She seems down-to-earth and that would appeal to Slade. She doesn't appear to relish dramatic, emotional scenes. She could've staged a dandy one when you showed up, but she didn't. And that's why you came over here tonight, isn't it, Lexie? For a grandstand performance. You love playing games and causing scenes and staging volatile quarrels, but that isn't what Slade wants. He's always been the calm and peace-loving one in the family and—"

"Oh, come off it, Vanessa," Lexie interrupted with a cynical little laugh. "The only reason you and your family are so hot for Slade to marry that girl is because she owns one-fourth of your damn mall! If I owned that property, you'd be just as eager to see me married to him, regardless of how right or wrong I am for him."

Shavonne realized she was holding her breath. She balled her hands into fists and stood stock-still, waiting for Vanessa's reply.

It was cool and concise. "But you don't own it, Lexie, and she does. So, she's marrying Slade with the Ramseys' heartfelt blessing."

Something that sounded like a sob escaped from Lexie. "I should've expected that from you! You Ramseys have b-bank vaults in the chambers of your hearts! But don't think I'm giving up, Vanessa. After you Ramseys have safely taken over that little fool's portion of the mall, I'm going to go after Slade again. The stakes will be even then. She won't have a twenty-five-million dollar advantage over me."

"Ah, the ultimate challenge, a married man. How dangerous, how exciting, how utterly Lexie." Vanessa's voice was laced with scorn. "Don't think it'll be easy, though, Lex. That little Shavonne is tenacious. From what we've learned about her, she's always had it hard and she's always toughed it out. Just think, a few weeks ago she was living in the pits of poverty and today she has the *Ramseys* groveling at her feet. You have to respect her for that."

Shavonne stared into space, the two women's words bouncing around in her head. They had each stated an important truth about her. One, she did have a twenty-five-million dollar advantage over Lexie Madison. And, two, she was tenacious.

She added two more truths to the list. She loved Slade, and she loved her family and was responsible for their welfare. Were all these things mutually exclusive, or could they somehow be integrated into the kind of life she wanted for herself, for Slade, and for her family?

Eleven

Shavonne was so preoccupied with her thoughts that she didn't hear Lexie and Vanessa exchange rather cool good-byes, nor did she hear Slade approaching her until he called out in a light, teasing voice, "So there you are! We were beginning to wonder what happened to you."

She started visibly, and when Slade reached her side, he pulled her into his arms. "I didn't mean to scare you, sweetheart." He wedged his knee between her thighs and molded her to him, asserting his possession. "What were you thinking about?" His tone had lost its lightness and his question sounded more like a command that had to be answered.

"A lot of things," she replied vaguely.

"Honey, I'm sorry that Lexie showed up here tonight." He nuzzled her neck. "But I want you to know that—"

"I wondered why Lexie looked so excited when she first came in" she interrupted absently, still pondering Vanessa's words. "It didn't occur to me that she was eagerly anticipating a big, emotional scene."

"Which she didn't get, much to her disappointment, I'm sure. Lexie has a flair for the dramatic which I find increasingly juvenile, exasperating, and exhausting. But you handled yourself beautifully, Shavonne." He pressed her closer. "With calm and pure class. The family has been talking about how much they admire you, honey. I, of course, admire you the most." He bent his head and took her mouth with his.

His kiss was hard and demanding, and just what she wanted. She wound her arms around his neck and kissed him ardently. Her body liquified as his hardened. His big hands caressed her gently, holding her closer, closer, but not close enough, not for either of them.

He lifted his head and muttered, "Come home with me, Shavonne."

She stared at him a little dazedly, and he laughed huskily. "I mean to my own house, where we'll be living after we're married." He traced her lips with the tip of his tongue. "We'll get you into Rice University. It's so near the house you can walk to some of your classes. Would you like that, Mrs. Ramsey?"

Mrs. Ramsey! Her heart spun at the sound. "If only it were that easy," she whispered, more to herself than to him, but he heard and kissed her fiercely.

"It is easy, sweetheart. We're going to be married and—"

"I hate to interrupt you two lovers, but the folks are getting nervous, wondering where you've run off to." The sound of Rad's voice caused Shavonne to draw back. Slade didn't release her though, and she remained securely within his embrace.

"So you were appointed a search party of one," Slade said dryly. "Tell the folks that there's nothing to be nervous about, Rad. Shavonne and I are just . . . talking privately."

"We really should rejoin them, Slade," she said hurriedly. She knew the unexpected appearance of Lexie Madison had unnerved all the Ramseys.

Slade groaned good-naturedly. "Okay, sweetie, but later . . ." He slipped his arm around her waist and turned to go back to the patio, but Rad stopped them.

"Just a minute, Slade, Shavonne."

He sounded nervous, and Shavonne gazed at him with curiosity. Slade had assured her that Rad, like his other siblings, was a decent person who could be quite warm, but that he hid that decency and warmth beneath a hard veneer of cynicism. The almost abashed expression of his face seemed totally out of character.

"Shavonne," he continued hesitantly, "I just wanted to say that I know we've treated you and your sisters and nieces poorly and that . . . Well, I just wanted to let you know . . ."

His voice trailed off, and Shavonne knew that was as close to an apology as she'd get from a Ramsey.

"Thank you, Rad," she said simply. "Shall we go now?"

Rad nodded with obvious relief and they all started down the hall together. As they walked Shavonne's thoughts were whirling, both from Rad's unexpected words and Vanessa and Lexie's conversation. Scraps of that conversation kept echoing in her mind, but one statement rang louder than all the others—*a twenty-five million dollar advantage.* There was no way to banish or deny Lexie's taunt. If she were to marry Slade, she would have to live with the painful uncertainty that her husband had married her under duress, and that there was another woman lying in wait for him when the odds had been evened. What kind of a marriage would that be? What kind of a life?

They reached the porch where the other family members were gathered. Vanessa had returned and gave Shavonne a bright smile. Two weeks ago Vanessa

Ramsey had been hurling china at the sight of the Bradys, Shavonne thought. Now she was perfectly willing to have one as a sister-in-law.

It was time to take charge of her life again, Shavonne decided as she smiled and nodded and made the appropriately pleasant comments in response to the Ramsey conversational blitz. She'd had two weeks of living in Fantasyland playing princess and it had been a wonderful break, but now she had to focus her energies on the future.

Since taking over as head of her family five years ago, she'd learned the necessity of sizing up a situation and acting out a solution. She'd just done the former, now it was time for the latter.

The Ramsey brothers were involved in a hot debate over the solutions to the Houston Oilers' woes on the football field, and she slipped from Slade's side to unobtrusively take a chair next to Quentin.

"May I speak to you privately for a few minutes?" she asked politely.

Quentin beamed and laid a paternal arm around her shoulders. "Sure, darlin', we'll step outside, hmm?" He led her from the terrace to the redwood deck overlooking the mammoth swimming pool. A shaft of moonlight reflected the big capital *R* inlaid in tiles in the bottom of the pool.

"This is a happy day for me, sugar," Quentin said warmly, taking her hand in his. "Seeing my boy settling down with—"

"—the beneficiary of your aunt Augusta's will," she finished dryly.

To his credit, Quentin made no disclaimer. "My father and my aunt were at odds my entire life." He shook his head, his expression puzzled. "I never did know what started their feud. My daddy wouldn't tell me. Sometimes I wonder if the two of them even remembered what it was. But they were both stubborn as mules, and hating each other got to be so ingrained . . ." He shrugged. "But that's all over with now, isn't it? Both of them are gone and—"

"It's not quite over," Shavonne interrupted. "It won't be over as long as I have the deed to Aunt Augusta's land." She drew in a deep breath. "That land is standing between Slade and me, and I want to be rid of it. Neither one of us will be free as long as I own it."

Quentin smiled broadly. "I understand, darlin'. I'll have my attorney draw up a transfer of ownership first thing in the morning."

Shavonne's smile was just as broad. "My attorney, Sissy Timmons, will handle the sale for me. I'll tell her that I don't want one penny more than the assessed value of the land."

"Sale?" Quentin repeated carefully. "Let's see if I heard you right, sugar. You plan to *sell* Ramsey and Sons this land? It's currently assessed at twenty-five million dollars—and that's what you intend to charge for it?"

"Mmm-hmm." She nodded and smiled pleasantly. And watched the older man's smile fade and his gray eyes grow cold as stones. *Eyes like a rattlesnake, and a disposition like one, too,* Augusta Ramsey had said of her brother Harlan. At this moment, that description fit Harlan's son as well, Shavonne thought firmly.

"Just a few weeks ago," he reminded her caustically, "you were willing to take twenty-five thousand dollars—rather than seventy-five—for that land because you thought it would mend a feud between Slade and me. What happened to that altruistic little gal? Been corrupted by wealth already, honey?"

"I don't think so." She shivered at the thought. "I hope not. But you have to admit that I'd be certifiable if I were to sell that property to you for twenty-five thousand dollars now that I know its true worth."

"And I'd be a fool to pay you even one thousand dollars for land which *should* be ours, little lady. Which *will* be ours just as soon as you marry my son." Quentin managed to put his smile back in place. "Now, you needn't worry that I'll mention your little extortion attempt to Slade, honey. And I won't hold it against you either. I know that hippie, pinko, fem-lib lawyer of yours is behind all this. We're going to get rid of her pronto. You're just an innocent little girl and—"

"Mr. Ramsey, I'm not a little girl. And I'm not guilty of extortion. *You* are." Her voice was calm but inside she was raging. "Augusta Ramsey left me that land to provide for my family. It would be the height of irresponsibility for me to simply hand it over to you."

"Your family." He frowned, as if suddenly remembering the existence of the rest of the Bradys. "Shoot, honey, if that's all that's bothering you, we can work something out. We'll arrange for them to receive some sort of monthly allowance until—"

"Something like a welfare check, you mean?" She was burning now. "Except instead of the government, Ramsey and Sons would be doling it out. On your terms and with plenty of strings attached. You'd be calling the shots in my sisters' lives. They'd have absolutely no freedom." It would be intolerable. She couldn't subject her family to such inevitable tyranny.

"Now, don't get huffy, sugar," he said in an attempt to placate her. "You'll be taken care of by Slade and we'll see to it that all the other girls marry well, too. Little girls don't need much money of their own when they have rich husbands to give them what they want."

Shavonne closed her eyes and counted to ten, then tacked on an additional twenty for good measure. Oh, Aunt Augusta, is this why you left Texas and your brother Harlan all those years ago? she silently asked her late benefactress. Because you didn't want to be a dependent little girl and the Ramsey conception of women was set in chauvinistic cement?

"Mr. Ramsey—"

"Quentin, darlin'. Unless you'd rather call me Daddy? Nola and I are looking forward to having another gal in the family. And Vanessa has always wanted a sister."

Shavonne refused to be diverted. "Mr. Ramsey, am I correct in assuming that you're refusing to buy the land?"

He grinned at her. "You sure are, honey. I'm not going to pay you a dime."

She stared bleakly at the water shimmering in the pool. There was no doubt about it, she was caught between the proverbial rock and a hard place.

"Don't worry your pretty little head about a thing, sugar." He gave her a fatherly squeeze. "You can't fight it. If a Ramsey wants something, a Ramsey gets it. Sort of the law of the land around here."

"And Augusta Ramsey wanted the Bradys to have her land," Shavonne said thoughtfully. How strange that the battle of wills between the irascible sister and brother should extend beyond the grave.

Slade joined them at that moment. He glanced from his father to Shavonne, noting her pensive expression and Quentin's triumphant grin, and had a sinking feeling in his chest.

Quentin greeted him exuberantly. "Slade! Your little bride and I were having a little get-acquainted chat." He pinched Shavonne's cheek playfully. "She's a real sweetheart."

Shavonne managed to smile. "I hope you'll always

feel that way about me, Quentin." She knew what she had to do and it involved laying to rest the Ramseys' treasured old maxim. Though it had never been formally put it into words, the Bradys, too, had a family motto, something along the lines of: A Brady did what had to be done.

Unfortunately, the two axioms clashed over the property issue, a fitting legacy from the warring Harlan and Augusta Ramsey. This Brady was about to do what had to be done. And that meant the Ramseys would not be getting what they wanted.

"Take you back to the hotel?" Slade was not at all happy to hear her request. "I want you to stay with me tonight. And you want it, too, love."

It was nearly midnight and they were in Slade's car, leaving River Oaks and the rest of the Ramseys.

"I'm exhausted, Slade."

"Then we'll go to bed and you can go right to sleep. You don't have to *entertain* me, Shavonne. I want you with me, even if it's simply holding you while you sleep."

She was touched, but remained firm. "Slade, I'd really prefer to—"

"I'm taking you home with me, Shavonne," he interrupted in a tone that brooked no argument.

Shavonne had that peculiar feeling of being trapped. The golden goose must not be allowed to slip away. She frowned. She didn't like it at all, this newly developed cynicism of hers. And the scene on the deck with Quentin had heightened her distrust. She had to put an end to it for Slade's sake, and her own.

"Slade, I was fairly good-natured about being kidnapped once tonight, but don't press your luck."

"Lexie's showing up like she did, upset you, didn't

it? That's the real reason why you won't spend the night with me. Sweetheart, for me there's absolutely no choice between you and her," he added fervently.

Her lips curved into a dry smile. "That's pretty much what Vanessa said, too."

"Well, Vanessa is absolutely right," Slade said firmly, and wondered how he could convince her of that fact. Shavonne was already insecure with him. Had Lexie's performance devastated any progress he'd made in rebuilding her trust? He silently cursed Lexie Madison and the day he'd met her. The woman had been nothing but trouble and misery for him, whereas Shavonne . . . Shavonne was warmth and sweetness and love.

And as much as he wanted her, taking her somewhere else against her will tonight wasn't going to prove to her that she could trust him, he admitted to himself with an inward sigh. He reached over and took her hand in his. "How about lunch tomorrow, then?"

"Yes, I'd like that," she said softly.

"And then we'll go shopping for your engagement ring." He lifted her hand to his lips and kissed her fingertips. "I want you to wear a visible sign that you belong to me. I'm a possessive man, Shavonne."

To his surprise, she didn't refuse to consider an outward symbol of the proposal she'd initially rejected. His hopes soared.

"I'm possessive, too, Slade," was her solemn reply. "Too possessive to ever share you with anyone."

"Darling, you'll never have to. I want you, only you."

Shavonne blinked back a sudden rush of tears. By lunchtime tomorrow, she would know for certain, one way or another. It was all a simple matter of doing what had to be done.

• • •

"Where shall we have lunch?" Shavonne asked Slade, as they walked hand-in-hand through the hotel lobby the next afternoon. "The food court in the mall?" It would be easier if there were lots of people and noise and activity around when she broke the news to him, she thought.

"I have a special place in mind," he said with an enigmatic smile. "It's private and it's quiet and the food is great—none of which you'll find at the mall food court."

She tensed. Private and quiet. She supposed it was only right. Serving him the news in the protective crowds of the food court was the coward's way out.

She was silent as they drove along the Loop, far too nervous to pay attention to where he was taking her. When he pulled to a stop in front of a big house on a shady, tree-lined street in a lovely, older neighborhood, she stared around in surprise. "Is this the restaurant?" she asked.

"This is my house, Shavonne." He came around the car to open her door for her. She'd been so quiet during the drive over here, he thought. Her apprehension was almost tangible. He stared at her, feeling his own tension knot in his stomach. Her refusal to stay with him last night suddenly portended ominously. Was this a more refined version of playing hard to get? Surely she wasn't going to turn down his proposal again? The terrible thought reverberated through him, and his expression turned grim.

He grasped her arm and silently led her up the walk.

"I thought we were going to have lunch," Shavonne said, gulping back the anxiety that had lodged like a boulder in her throat.

"I have a freezer full of frozen entrees, from pizza to chicken kiev. I'm sure you'll find something that appeals to you."

She stole a quick glance at him. He sounded almost angry. Her heart, already thudding, ripped into jackhammer speed. This wouldn't be easy if he were in the most jovial of spirits. But if he were already mad at her . . .

Had Quentin told him of her attempts to sell the land? she wondered. And if so, did he share his father's feelings that she had been out of line to offer to sell, not give her inheritance to the Ramseys? Her qualms grew.

Slade guided her inside the house, through a large tiled entranceway, and into a spacious, modern kitchen. Under normal circumstances, she would have admired the ample counter space, the gleaming appliances, and sunny breakfast nook. But these were not normal circumstances.

Taking a deep breath, she reached into her purse and pulled out the legal document she had watched Sissy Timmons draft, the one that had been signed and notarized this morning. Her hands were shaking.

"Slade, first I want to tell you that—that I love you and I mean to marry you."

Her breathless declaration had an instant effect upon Slade. His head jerked up and he stared at her for a moment, as if he didn't believe what he had heard. Then he caught her around the waist and pulled her to him, his face alight with joy. "Shavonne, oh, sweetheart, do you know how happy you've made me?"

The papers fluttered to the floor as his arms encircled her. "Darling, now I understand why you've been so nervous with me today." His eyes were tender as he gazed down at her. "You decided to quit playing and respond honestly and openly to me. And in light of your past history, I know what a perilous risk you feel you're taking."

She stared up at him, bewilderment momentarily

eplacing her tension. Then she stooped to gather
p the papers, and her anxiety returned.

"Honey, what's wrong?" he asked, reaching for
er again.

Her entire body quivered. It was now or never.
Slade, I want you to read this." She thrust the
apers into his hands. "And—And I want you to know
hat I understand if you'd rather not marry me after
eading it . . ." Her voice trailed off as she watched
is eyes flick over the opening paragraph.

Her legs were shaking too much to stand. As Slade
ontinued to read, she made her way to the kitchen
able and sank into one of the bright blue and white
hairs.

He joined her there a few minutes later. He sat in
he chair across from her and laid the document on
he table in front of her. She reached for it with icy
ingers. She wanted to say something, but she
ouldn't think of a single thing. Nor could she look
t Slade. He hadn't said a word and the silence
oomed between them. She thought of the noisy
andemonium of the mall food court and wished
hey were there right now.

"According to these papers," he said at last, "your
ister Erin now holds the deed to the land you in-
erited from Great-Aunt Augusta."

"I didn't sign over everything to Erin," she cor-
ected him. "Trust funds are to be set up for Tara,
Colleen, Megan, Carrie Beth, and Courtney. And for
ne, too. That way none of us will be financially
lependent on anyone, not even each other. The rest
s in Erin's name with Sissy Timmons serving as
inancial adviser and administrator of the trusts
nd estate."

He was silent, staring at the document.

"You're probably wondering why I did it," she said,
wisting the paper with nervous fingers. "I didn't

want to take such drastic action, but when your father refused to buy the land . . ."

Slade made no response and she forced herself to continue. "I couldn't let my sisters depend on your family's charity, not when I had the means to provide for them. You don't know what it's like to be poor, but we do. Poverty isn't ennobling or redeeming. I think the rich put that out to keep the poor in line. Being dirt poor is hard, and it can be scary and demeaning, too. Anyone who's ever had to worry about how to pay their next bill would understand why I couldn't just give you the land because I love you and cast our fate to the wind. I *had* to make sure my family was taken care of. I—I wish I could've handed you that deed believing that we would all live on love, but . . . Oh, Slade, this sounds terribly unromantic and depressingly practical, but I just couldn't afford such a gesture. Not with six people depending on me."

"And you didn't feel you could explain any of this to me? You didn't think to come to me for help?"

Tears burned her eyes. "I knew the pressure you were under from your family. I was under the same sort of pressure. We both had to look out for our families in our own way. Neither of us could be free to make a choice. Until now."

"My choice was made when I asked you to marry me, Shavonne."

She swallowed hard. "That was when I had a twenty-five-million dollar incentive bonus attached to me. I don't consider that a free choice, Slade. Nobody would."

The silence between them seemed to stretch on endlessly, but a glance at the kitchen clock showed Shavonne that only a minute or two had passed.

Then Slade asked, "Do you realize what you've done, Shavonne?"

Was he questioning if she was of sound mind when she'd signed the document? she wondered. Would a team of Ramsey attorneys challenge her to a competency test? The prospect was too grim to bear.

He reached over and covered her hand with his, his fingers interlocking with hers. "You've made Erin the hottest matrimonial prospect in town. Rad, Jed, Troy Timmons—those are just three who are certain to beat a path to her door."

Shavonne dared to look up at him. He was smiling! Her heart took flight. "That's all you're going to say?" She struggled to come to terms with what seemed to be happening. "You're not going to tell me I'm crazy for giving up a fortune."

"You're not crazy." He smiled wryly. "And you're not terribly unromantic or depressingly practical, either. You're generous and realistic and responsible. But I wish you would have told me your concerns about your family because I could have assured you that I would never let my father take that land from you without paying full value."

He stroked her palm with his thumb in an intimate little caress that somehow was as soothing as it was arousing. "I do understand why you didn't tell me. You're used to taking on everything by yourself. But not any more, sweetheart. It may take some time, but you're going to learn that I'll always be there for you, always on your side."

"You don't hate me for not giving the land to your family?" she whispered.

"Shavonne, when you told me you wanted to marry me, you made me the happiest man in the world. Nothing has changed since that moment."

"Oh, Slade!" She fairly floated to his side and threw her arms around his neck.

He pulled her down onto his lap. His arms embraced her and he kissed her deeply, his tongue seeking hers. When they parted, her eyes were shining and her cheeks were suffused with color. "Did you actually think I would be angry with you, love?" he asked.

She cuddled closer, shivering a little at that unpleasant prospect. "There was always that possibility."

"You thought I wanted to marry you to get the land." He shook his head. "I should've guessed that was behind your hesitation, but your sisters threw me off the track when they told me you were playing hard to get."

"Playing hard to get?" she laughed. "Hardly! I melted every time you touched me. I thought it was incredibly obvious that you didn't have to get me. You had me." Her arms were curled around his neck. She stroked the nape of his neck with her finger.

"I wanted to believe that, but I'd already made so many mistakes with you. I love you so much and I couldn't face the risk of losing you. I thought once we were safely married, I could show you how much I cared without having to worry about—" He paused and frowned.

"About what?" She demanded, bending down to kiss his neck.

"My mother came tearing into my office with tales of Troy Timmons and his plans to sweep you off your feet. I panicked." He brushed a light kiss across her mouth. "I hurt you badly two years ago, sweetheart. That's a strike against me that another man wouldn't have to overcome."

She hugged him reassuringly. "I've always wanted you, Slade, you're the only man I've ever wanted." Then she tilted her head and gave him an incredulous look. "Troy Timmons? Good heavens, Slade, I just met the man last night!" She chuckled. "So that's why you whisked me away so fast?"

"And compounded my mistake by taking you to my parents' house." He groaned in remembrance.

They were about as subtle as a nuclear explosion. And when Lexie showed up . . ."

"She made me realize that I had to do something, Slade," Shavonne said earnestly. "By then I knew an affair with you would never be enough. I wanted to marry you. So I evened out the odds. I figured that if I didn't have a quarter-share of the Ramsey Park Mall, you could choose freely."

"Sweetheart, I chose freely a long time ago. You're my dream girl. You're everything I've always wanted in a woman." He paused to kiss her. "And a lover." Another kiss. "And a wife."

"Lexie said she was going to go after you after we were married." Shavonne warned, her dark eyes flashing as she remembered the other woman's bold assertion.

Slade grinned at her. "Thank God I'll have you to protect me from that airhead! And I can guarantee she'll lose interest awfully fast when she realizes that I'm a happily married man, devoted to his wife. Shavonne, whatever I felt for Lexie—and I'm sure it wasn't love—is long dead. You can be certain of that."

His response was everything she could have hoped for, convincing Shavonne beyond a question of a doubt that she had nothing to fear from any other woman, especially his former fiancée.

"I love you, Slade." Her lips moved across his cheek to his mouth and she kissed him, hungrily, urgently, with all the passion of a woman in love.

"And I love you." He stood up, lifting her high against his chest. He was smiling at her in a way that made her feel wonderfully cherished and loved. "Shall we go to bed now, or are you set on having lunch first?"

"Suppose I choose lunch?" she teased, playfully running a finger over his lips.

He shoot her a baleful glare that made her giggle. "I just changed my mind," she said, "let's go to bed."

He rewarded her with a kiss. Then he was carrying her through the house, up a wide staircase, and into a large bedroom, which was done in shades of navy and forest green. "Is this your room?" she asked dreamily as he laid her down on the bed.

"Our room," he corrected her. "The girls' bedrooms are on the other side of the landing and we have our own bath, so we'll have plenty of privacy." His fingers unfastened the buttons of her blouse with remarkable speed. "I know your sisters and your nieces will be living with us, honey, so you needn't worry about how to spring it on me."

She gazed at him. "To tell you the truth, I hadn't gotten that far. I wasn't sure if you'd dump me for dumping the mall on Erin, remember?"

"There was never a chance of that. Meanwhile," he went on enthusiastically, "I've been making plans. I've asked about Colleen and Megan attending the same private high school as my brother Ricky and their admission seems guaranteed. And we can arrange for Tara to transfer to a college here in Texas if she wants to be near the family."

"I think she'd like that," Shavonne said softly. "But I'm sure she'd like even more to live on campus. It'll be her first chance to have a real social life."

"Whatever she wants. As for Erin, well, you've given her unlimited options. She and the babies are certainly welcome to live here with us."

"There are just a couple more loose strings to tie up," Shavonne murmured, her senses stirring as he seductively rubbed his mouth against hers. "Will your family ever forgive me for not bringing that quarter of the mall as my dowry?"

His mouth curved into a resolute smile, and he looked as determined and unyielding and formidable as any Ramsey. "I promise you're going to be welcomed and loved, Shavonne," he said firmly.

Her eyes sparkled with happiness. "After all," she added cheekily, "as the sister of the new owner of one-quarter of the Ramsey Park Mall, I might prove to be invaluable."

"You *are* invaluable, Shavonne. Loving you has made me the happiest, luckiest man in the world," Slade said softly.

"Which just goes to prove that in the end, nice guys win after all," she murmured, and claimed his mouth in a kiss that said it all.

THE EDITOR'S CORNER

In celebration of our first anniversary we printed the following in our Editor's Corner—"It seems only a breathless moment ago that we launched LOVESWEPT into the crowded sea of romance publishing." Many things have happened in the years since we published the first LOVESWEPTs. The market has seen the birth of new romance lines and, sad to say, the demise of romance lines. Through it all we have remained true to the statement we made in our first anniversary issue—"Each time we've reached the goal of providing a truly fresh, creative love story, we find our goal expands, and we have a new standard of freshness and creativity to strive for." We try. Sometimes we don't hit on the mark. Sometimes we astonish even ourselves by hitting it square in the center. But thanks to the support of each of you, all the LOVESWEPT authors are growing and learning, while doing what we most like and want to do. We have even more of a challenge in presenting not just four, but six terrific romances each month.

It is such a pleasure to have a Helen Mittermeyer love story to kick off our expanded list next month. In **KISMET,** LOVESWEPT #210, Helen gives you another of her tempestuous romances with a heroine and hero who match each other in passion and emotional intensity. Tru Hubbard meets Thane Stone at one of the most difficult times in her life—certainly not the time to fall head-over-heels in love. Yet she does, and it looks as if she's rushing headlong into another emotionally disastrous situation, not just for herself, but for Thane, too. And so she runs as far and as fast as she can. But she's failed to realize her man is ready to walk through fire for her. A very exciting love story!

If there's a city more romantic than Paris, someone has failed to let me know. I think you'll love the setting almost as much as the heroine and hero in Kathleen Downes's LOVESWEPT #211, **EVENINGS IN PARIS.** From the moment Bart Callister spies a lovely mystery woman on the deck of the Eiffel Tower until he has pursued and caught lovely Arri Smith there's breathless, mysterious love and romance to charm you. But Arri's afraid. She knows she's no siren! You'll relish the ways that Bart handles her when she thinks *all* her secrets have been revealed. A true delight!

It is a great pleasure for me to introduce you to our new author Margie McDonnell and her poignant romance **BANISH THE DRAGONS,** LOVESWEPT #212. I had the pleasure of working with Margie before I came to Bantam, so I know she writes truly from knowledge of the heart and of courage, traits

(continued)

that she shows in her own life. Here she brings you a captivating couple, David and Angela, who know the worst that life has to offer and whose bravery and optimism and head-over-heels love will make you sing for joy, when you're not cheering them—and the children they deal with in a very special summer camp. A truly heartwarming, memorable debut.

Sit back, relax, and prepare to chuckle with glee and thrill to romance as you read Joan Elliott Pickart's **LEPRECHAUN, LOVESWEPT #213**. Imagine Blake Pemberton's shock when, home sick with the flu, a woman appears at his bedside who is so sprightly and lovely she seems truly to be one of the "little people" of Irish legend. And imagine Nichelle Clay's shock when she shows up to clean an apartment and confronts a sinfully gorgeous hunk wrapped in one thin sheet! A charming romp, first to last.

Welcome back Olivia and Ken Harper with **A KNIGHT TO REMEMBER, LOVESWEPT #214**. Tegan Knight sizzles with surprises for hero Jason Sloane, who is sure the T in her first name stands for Trouble. She'd do just about anything to thwart his business plans, but she hadn't counted on his plans for her! And those she cannot thwart—but what red-blooded woman would even want to? Two devilishly determined charmers make for one great romance.

LOVING JENNY, LOVESWEPT #215, showcases the creativity and talent of Billie Green. There are very few authors who could pull off what Billie does in this incredible story. Her heroine, Jenny Valiant, crashes her ex-husband's wedding reception to inform him their quickie divorce was as valid as a three dollar bill. Then she whisks him away (along with his bride) to sunny Mexico for another, but this time valid divorce, and sweeps them all into one of the most tender, touching, humorous romances of all time. A fabulous love story.

Enjoy!

Carolyn Nichols

Carolyn Nichols
    Editor

LOVESWEPT
Bantam Books, Inc.
666 Fifth Avenue
New York, NY 10103